D1360343

Everybody Loved Roger Harden

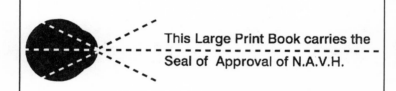

This Large Print Book carries the
Seal of Approval of N.A.V.H.

EVERYBODY'S SUSPECT IN GEORGIA,
BOOK 1

EVERYBODY LOVED ROGER HARDEN

A ROMANCE MYSTERY

CECIL MURPHEY

THORNDIKE PRESS

A part of Gale, Cengage Learning

Detroit • New York • San Francisco • New Haven, Conn • Waterville, Maine • London

LIBRARY OF CONGRESS CATALOGING-IN-PUBLICATION DATA

Murphey, Cecil.
    Everybody loved Roger Harden : a romance mystery / by Cecil Murphey.
        p. cm. — (Thorndike Press large print Christian mystery)
    (Everybody's suspect in Georgia ; v bk. 1)
    ISBN-13: 978-1-4104-2223-1 (hardcover : alk. paper)
    ISBN-10: 1-4104-2223-2 (hardcover : alk. paper)
    1. Women psychologists—Fiction. 2. Clergy—Fiction. 3. Philanthropists—Crimes against—Fiction. 4. Georgia—Fiction. 5. Large type books. I. Title.
PS3613.U723E94 2009
813'.6—dc22   2009034567

Published in 2009 by arrangement with Barbour Publishing, Inc.

Printed in the United States of America
1 2 3 4 5 6 7 13 12 11 10 09

Thanks to members of the Bible Discovery Class and to my wonderful agents, Steve Laube and Deidre Knight. Most of all, my love and thanks to Shirley.

1

When I agreed to attend Roger Harden's dinner party, how could I have known the terrible events that would take place on Palm Island and especially what would happen to Roger himself? I also had no idea that anyone would find out about my past. Roger knew, of course, but imagine — me *voluntarily* telling everyone my long-held secret.

Sorry, there I go again. I'm getting ahead of myself. I do that a lot. I start telling a story and jump ahead to the best parts. I'll try not to do that again. I've promised myself that I would write everything down exactly as it happened. So I can't reveal anything about what took place on Palm Island before I reached Roger's house, can I?

I'm Julie West, and I decided to write down all the strange occurrences on Palm Island so that I don't forget anything.

There's one part that Burton needs to explain because I wasn't there. I asked him to note those events, exactly as I'm trying to do.

So here is how it happened. I had barely reached the dockside, and it was exactly 7:51. It was late June, and the breeze along the Georgia coast made the evenings cool enough for a sweater or light jacket. I had worn a windbreaker and slacks, so I was all right. Sure, my hair was a mess, but everyone expected that. Because I keep my titian-colored hair short and it's naturally curly, a comb was all I'd need anyway.

I was more concerned about the time than my hair. When Roger said eight o'clock for dinner, he meant everyone was to be present, seated, hands in their laps, and silent — totally silent — when the large hall clock struck the hour. I knew the ritual: I'd been to dinner there three times previously.

If anyone was late, Roger never said anything. He didn't need to. His pale blue eyes glared in a way that made words unnecessary. Each time, I felt like a fourth grader on my first day of school when the teacher's roving eyes intimidated me.

I would have arrived at the dock at least fifteen minutes earlier if it hadn't been for the heavy traffic along I-95. There must have been an accident near Savannah. Although I never saw the collision, I got jammed up in the snarled, stop-and-start trail of automobiles.

When I finally arrived at the dock and caught sight of the boat, I sighed with relief, knowing I could reach the island in time. After I shut off the car engine at the dockside, I hurried around to the trunk of my Honda hybrid.

A man I didn't recognize struggled to get his suitcase wedged into the specially built hold on Roger Harden's prized Boston Whaler. Alongside him, Simon Presswood, Roger's handyman, pulled the bag from the man's hand and deftly twisted the bulky suitcase so it slid with ease into the special compartment.

"I need a little help over here," I called to Simon.

He got out of the Boston Whaler and came over to me. When he reached my car, he shrugged.

I shrugged in return, but Simon ignored me. He walked directly to my opened car trunk and picked up the heaviest of my bags. He then offered his arm to help me into the Whaler.

This time Roger hadn't come along, which was unusual. He loved to give his guests such a detailed explanation of his boat, it almost sounded as if he had designed and built the craft himself. For someone like me, it was more fun to observe his excitement than it was to listen to him talk about a two-hundred-horsepower Mercury Verado four-cycle engine. He hated it when anyone called it a motor — as if the person had used profane language.

At the beginning of my two previous trips, Roger had lectured us as he pointed out the remarkable features of the boat. "It will still float, even if ten people are inside and it's filled with water." (I refrained from asking him why ten people would stay inside a water-filled boat. Why wouldn't they bail with their life jackets on?) Both times I cringed when he pointed out that the boat could withstand a thousand rounds of automatic weapon fire. That statement always puzzled me. Unless, of course, he expected South American terrorists to pursue him.

The Boston Whaler was about eight feet wide, big enough to keep us dry, and it had an engine that worked well. Okay, it was nice to look at, and the boat shouted quality and money, but to me, a boat is a boat. On my previous trips, during Roger's lectures, I'd stared at the ocean vessels streaming across the Atlantic while he droned on. Or I'd gazed at the sea oats along the sand dunes. Only about six inches tall (with roots as long as five feet), the sea oats not only protect the dunes from erosion, but I like to think they wave at me.

I thought it was funny when Roger condescended and treated us like idiots, so I referred to the Whaler as a "rowboat with a motor."

Roger didn't have a great sense of humor. He reminded me that the Whaler was "very stable, very dry, and very comfortable." He clasped his hands behind his back. "And it has an engine, *not* a motor."

On my first trip, another passenger added, "It's a quality boat for the obscenely rich."

Roger loved that remark, indicated by the swell of his chest. "Quite right," he'd say. Yes, Roger liked to give his guests the best.

But today Roger wasn't present, and Simon was ready to leave. He had tied the Whaler to the small dock so no one had to get wet climbing inside.

Without going into details of the boring introduction, the stranger's name was Dr. James Burton, the minister at a church in Riverdale in Clayton County on Atlanta's Southside — about ten minutes' drive from my office. He told me he had arrived at the dock in Brunswick at 7:20 — the time I was supposed to have gotten there. He mentioned that I was the last to arrive.

If I had driven in by 7:20, that would have given us plenty of time to board the Whaler and arrive on Palm Island long before 8:00.

I didn't blame the minister for being irritated, though he didn't say anything overtly negative. His frown told me he wasn't happy at being delayed.

I thanked Simon for helping me. He's tall — about half a foot over six feet — and always keeps his head shaved. I never could figure out why, because he doesn't have that slick bald scalp that most men do who shave their heads. He has a large, barely visible scar on the left side of his face, running from his temple to the top of his lip. Simon would make a frightening appearance with his broad shoulders, dark coloring, and huge eyebrows — except for his soft brown eyes. When he looked at me, I felt as if he were like a small boy trapped inside a huge body. He never revealed anything about himself and always ignored any personal questions. I assumed he didn't understand English well because he rarely spoke. Mostly he shrugged or answered in terse statements.

"Are all the others here?" I asked.

Simon nodded.

"How many are on the island?"

He shrugged. "Nine. Also Mrs. Harden. Jason." (Jason was Roger's stepson).

"He go," Simon said, his chin jutted out to point to the man already seated in the red boat.

Dr. Burton, or as he informed us with a grin that showed a set of teeth a Hollywood movie star would envy, said, "Just call me Burton. Everyone does."

"I'm sorry I'm late." I laughed self-consciously and said, "Just like a woman, huh?"

"You want to blame your whole gender because you're late?"

"Just trying to make it a joke," I said. "Traffic problem around Savannah."

"Hmm," he said.

"Or maybe I should blame it on the way we women drive or —"

"Or that you could have started earlier."

"Tide soon full. Wait no longer." Simon shrugged.

It was my turn to shrug. This time his back was to me and he didn't see my action. I like doing that with Simon. Sometimes he smiles when I imitate his gestures, especially the way he uses his chin to point at an object. It's better than using fingers, I guess. I love that chin thing; it's his best gesture.

"We're ready," I said to Simon and smiled at Burton. I knew it wouldn't do any good to smile at Simon.

Burton sat on the far right side of the Whaler as if he wanted to give me three-fourths of the seat. I moved to the far left and figured a third person and perhaps a fourth could have sat between us. Instead, we both put our life jackets in the empty space even though we knew we were supposed to wear them.

I could write another couple of pages about Dr. James Burton. I knew he was irritated — and as I was to learn, that wasn't typical of him. He certainly had a right to be upset. I was upset at myself for being so late.

Besides his perfect teeth, Burton is all-around good-looking. I'm five ten in my sneakers, and he was maybe less than an inch shorter. He wasn't wearing a wedding ring, and that made him look even better. I liked his dark eyes and those fabulous dark curls. He had two short ringlets right in the middle of his forehead. He was trim, and his arms made him look like a weight lifter. He didn't have that football belly I'd seen in so many men his age — around thirty, I figured — and I liked that about him.

Burton tried to talk to Simon as the engine caught hold and the Whaler pulled away from the shore. The ride was noisy, of course, but I could hear Burton's questions easily enough. The answers came back with shrugs, nods, or shaking of the head. Simon was, well, just Simon.

Palm Island was originally an isthmus, but billionaire Roger Harden had the land dug away from the mainland because he wanted isolation, and he got it. The gossip I heard said that isolation had cost him somewhere around twelve million dollars. I don't know what power he had to exert to make the isthmus an island, but he did, and I assume part of those millions was to influence the right officials and politicians. Roger told me that once he separated it from the mainland, he had to give it a name, and he called it Palm Island. He laughed and said, "I planted three palm trees."

In the late 1990s, he had spent more money — a lot more money — to install an underground land telephone line. The telephone worked about 60 percent of the time.

"Any Internet access from here?" Burton asked. "I brought my laptop. I thought I might use it."

"If the phone works."

"If the phone doesn't?"

Simon shrugged. "In two weeks, Wi-Fi."

"Cell phones? They work here?"

This time I laughed. "About 1 percent of the time. Roger tried to explain it to me once, but I never understood the reason. Right, Simon?"

Simon shrugged.

Just then, Simon nosed the Whaler expertly to the small dock at the island, turned off the engine, and jumped out. He held up his hand for Burton to remain seated. Simon was barefooted and wore loose, pale green shorts and a brown shirt that hung almost to the bottom of his shorts. From the side of the boat, he leaned forward, grabbed a rope from the dock, and effortlessly pulled the Whaler the last few feet. "Out," he said. "Suitcases I bring."

The tide was rising fast, and I realized there was almost no beach left. Now I understood what Simon had meant about no time. In a few minutes, the fierce waves would have made it impossible to settle at the small dock, a T-shaped walkway.

Simon jumped out and reached down to give me a hand. Once out of the Whaler, I hurried across the ten-foot walkway and up the steps. From the top, I paused to look into the west. I loved to watch the sun move slowly toward the horizon. I'm not one of those nature freaks, but sights at the coast dazzle me. Bright steams of red and gold sneaked across the sky as if they wanted to make an announcement of sunset. Dark clouds appeared in the east as if to promise rain before morning.

I looked at my watch. It was 7:58. "Hurry. Roger hates it when anyone is late."

Behind me, Burton stumbled, so I grabbed his hand, and we raced toward the front entrance.

"If I was rude to you," he yelled, "I'm sorry."

"You were rude, but it's all right because I didn't hear you," I yelled back to him as we raced ahead. I love it when I can give smart-mouthed answers.

I didn't knock but pushed the door open. We hurried through the foyer and straight toward the dining room, which was perhaps thirty feet and to the left. The minute hand on the large antique clock showed 7:59. I sighed and released Burton's hand. We paused, and I smiled at him as he stepped back and I walked sedately into the room. I liked the feel of his hand — smooth but strong. Very masculine. I caught the barest whiff of his cologne — a strong, manly fragrance.

Several people attempted to smile at us — or perhaps they only grimaced. I didn't know anyone except Amanda Harden and her son, Jason. She indicated the place for me on her right, which left one space for Burton directly across the table and next to Jason. I liked that because I could look at Burton without being rude.

The host's chair, of course, was empty.

"Hello, everyone," I said as my gaze swept around the table. "I'm Julie West from Atlanta."

Across from me and down one on my right, a heavyset man smiled at me. "Hi there! Welcome to Palm Island! I'm Lenny Goss. This is my first time to meet with such a fun group of people." He laughed as he lifted his hand in a kind of handshaking gesture. He looked around, but no one responded to his "fun group of people." His smile melted into a small pout.

No one else spoke or acknowledged me, but I wasn't surprised. After all, this was Roger Harden's house, and he knew exactly what he wanted. Obviously, the others — except Lenny — had been well trained. None of us could see the large clock in the hallway, but I knew everyone strained to hear its ticking. Like most of them, I had been to Palm Island before, so I understood Roger's odd behavior. It was simple: He did not want to hear any talking when he made his grand entrance into the immense dining room. I thought it was a bit eccentric but decided that when a man's net worth is somewhere in the low billions, he could act as nutty as he wanted.

The absolute silence seemed a bit weird and silly, but it was his house and we were his guests.

No one else said a word. Just then the wind began to huff at the windows, and somewhere a loose shutter banged. I had checked the weather on the Internet before I left; the experts predicted rain before midnight along the coast.

Burton started to say something to the middle-aged woman on his right. But she put her long, red-nailed index finger to her lips.

Lenny's eyes darted toward a tall bottle-blond across from him. She looked vaguely familiar. Her thick hair had fallen across one eye. She pushed it away with her tapered and perfectly formed fingers. They were natural nails and painted a light pink. She wore a pink cotton-blend blouse and a dark blue Chanel suit, and her nails matched the shade of her blouse. *Nice touch,* I thought.

Without trying to be obvious, I looked closely at Amanda, one of the most strikingly beautiful women I'd ever seen. She wore tight-fitting gold silk pants and a matching low-cut, cowl-neck, satin blouse that probably cost more than I earned in a month. Her shoulder-length golden earrings and heavy gold chain seemed a little overdone, even for Roger's house. About a year ago she started dyeing her hair — and it looked great — into a slightly lighter shade of ash-blond than her natural color. I couldn't detect one bit of gray. Amanda had always been trim and beautiful, although I noticed the seams of her silk pants now strained when she shifted her weight. She must have added ten pounds since I'd seen her last. She smiled at me, but it seemed slightly forced.

While the other guests waited in silence, Burton looked across at me and arched his right brow. I shrugged in a perfect Simon-like gesture. He returned the Simon shrug — not quite perfect, but he'd get it right before we left.

I put my napkin on my lap and imitated everyone by sitting with my hands folded. The seconds ticked away. We had fourteen seconds to go. I sighed in relief. I had made it on time.

As we waited, I tried not to look around, because I never liked Roger's taste in furniture. Everything in the house was done in the rococo style. While Roger thought it exuded delicacy and lightness — which I suppose it did — I thought it was too elaborately ornamented with shell motifs, serpentine curves, and cabriole legs, and not particularly comfortable. Finely done needlepoint of floral designs cushioned the seats and chair backs. I used to tell him I'd rather look at his chairs than sit on them. He didn't like that part of my humor, either.

The grandfather clock began its first clang.

No one moved. I closed my eyes so that I didn't laugh. We were all adults, all sitting in stiff obedience like kids in a military school. But then, that was Roger's way.

Silently I counted the gongs. Surreptitiously, I looked around at the other guests. Across the table from me sat a fiftyish-looking woman whose lips moved silently as she also counted. She had one of those severe hairstyles — hair pulled back into a bun — and she wore thick, dark-framed glasses. Later I learned her name was Tonya Borders, Roger's longtime lawyer. She looked like a woman who had forgotten how

21

to smile. But then, I reasoned, maybe the poor woman had nothing to smile about.

The clock finished chiming.

Our eyes automatically turned toward the open door, which was only feet from Roger's office. This was the moment for his appearance — just as the clock struck its eighth and final gong.

Roger didn't come into the room.

For several seconds, no one spoke a word, but all of us turned toward Amanda as if on cue.

"Where is Roger?" she asked no one in particular. "He is never late." She rang the small bell beside her plate.

A tall, rail-thin woman in a maid's uniform appeared immediately. She carried a soup tureen. "Where is Mr. Harden?" Amanda asked.

"I do not know, mum. I'll go check on him."

Her name was Elaine Wright, and she had been with the Hardens for about four years. Elaine turned back into the kitchen with the soup. We could hear her set it on the stove or a ledge, and seconds later, she crossed the room and left by the other door. She wore a type of backless shoe that made every footstep echo through the dining room. She knocked on the door of Roger's study.

A few seconds later, we heard her knock again. More like pounding the door this time. "Mr. Harden? Are you in there, sir?" Her tone was a notch below panicked.

"Sir? I'm coming in now." Apparently, she then opened the office door.

She screamed.

2

After Mrs. Wright's scream, we all hurried out of the dining room, rushed into the hall, and turned left. Elaine Wright stood at the door and pointed. "Mr. Harden — he is — he is — something has happened to Mr. Harden!"

Burton pushed past her and entered the office, and the rest of us followed.

Roger lay on his back on the floor behind his desk. A pool of blood stained his face and his shirt, and blood had dripped onto the floor.

Burton squatted then pressed two fingers to Roger's neck. "No pulse," he said. "I'm no expert, but I'd say that looks as if he's been shot." He pointed to what was obviously a gunshot wound in his temple.

Amanda brushed past me. She didn't kneel — not in those form-fitting silk pants — but she bent over, and it was obvious she was genuinely shocked. "Shot? Who would want to do that?" She turned around and stared at us. "Who would — who would want to kill him? Why would any of you — ?"

Although all of us had hurried toward the office, I was the last one to enter. Just then, Simon walked into the house with our luggage. I turned around and heard the thump of our suitcases. He raced past me and pushed several people out of the way. "No! No!"

The next few minutes remain jumbled in my mind while we tried to adjust to the shock of Roger's death. Somebody screamed, and I heard wails of "It can't be! It can't be!"

"He was my best friend, my best friend," moaned a balding man in glasses. He put his right hand under his glasses to wipe his eyes. I couldn't be sure, because I couldn't see clearly from where I stood, but I don't think he actually shed tears even though he made a big show of wiping his face.

There was so much noise and talking and groaning, I don't remember anything else distinctly until Simon hurried out of the office and down the hallway. Seconds later he returned with two dark blankets. "Go," he said and covered the body without moving it. It was only an impression I had, but the gentleness with which he covered Harden's body appeared more genuine and heartfelt than any other response I had observed.

The one exception was Jason Harden. I wasn't sure, but he seemed to show genuine grief. He made no noise, but tears slid silently down his cheeks.

Burton took over and quietly got us all back into the dining room. I don't remember how he did that, but he had obviously taken charge.

I stood by the door and didn't move until everyone was gone. Simon remained by Roger's body. He came out last.

"Lock door," he said and pulled a key from his pocket. He turned and put the key into the lock.

The others whispered to each other, but I heard more than one person say, "Why? Everybody loved Roger Harden."

"What reason would anyone have to kill dear Roger?" one of the women asked.

Once we had returned to the dining room, we stood around awkwardly. No one seemed to want to sit at the table.

"If he was shot, surely one of you heard the noise," Burton said. He pointed to me. "Julie and I arrived with Simon less than a minute before the clock began to chime. The rest of you were here." He turned to

Mrs. Wright and asked, "Is there anyone else on the island?"

"Just the eleven of you, as well as Simon and me."

"His body is still warm, so it must have happened recently."

They began to stare at each other, raise eyebrows, and make quiet protestations as if they didn't want poor Roger to hear them discuss details.

"I would never hurt Roger." I don't remember who said that, but it was one of the men.

Burton turned to the maid and said, "Uh, sorry, I don't know your name, but —"

"My name is Elaine Wright."

"Okay, Elaine, please —"

"Mrs. Wright, if you please."

"Sorry. Mrs. Wright, will you call the police?"

"I shall use the extension in the kitchen." She left the dining room.

"While we wait, I wonder if anyone has any information about Roger that would shed light on this."

"Everybody loved Roger Harden," said a woman in her midthirties who identified herself as Paulette White. She was overdressed in a black poufy dress and overjeweled with three strands of pearls. Her bouffant hair seemed as if it had been glued to her scalp. "No one would ever want to harm him. Why, he's such a kind man, and he's done so much good for the community, and —"

"The phone is out again," Mrs. Wright announced from the doorway.

"How long has it been out?" Burton asked. "Do you have any idea?"

"Phone rang two hours ago," Simon said.

"Yes, that is correct," the maid answered. "It rang just a couple of minutes before or after 6:00. I was clearing up the last of the tea dishes. By the time I reached the kitchen, Mr. Harden had picked up the phone in his office."

"Did you overhear what Mr. Harden said?" Burton asked.

"Certainly not," she replied. "I would not do such a thing." She stared at Burton as if she dared him to challenge her.

"If I offended you, I apologize," Burton said. "I assume you heard his voice when he first spoke to the other person."

"It was a man on the other end, and he said, 'All right.' Then Mr. Harden said something to the effect that it was not an appropriate time to call. I hung up the phone in the kitchen."

"So that means he must have been killed

some time after 6:15."

"He was alive at 7:00," said a man with a deep voice. He was paunchy, probably about sixty, with blotchy skin. He might have been handsome once, but that could only have been before his second birthday. He had a bulbous nose, large ears, and deep-set brown eyes. He wore those old-fashioned tortoise-colored glasses that made him look as if he had worn the same pair since about 1970.

"And who are you?" Burton asked. "I don't know any of you except Jason and Amanda."

"My name is Wayne Holmestead," he said in a low, deep voice that probably scared employees. "I have known that kind, generous, and wonderful man for nearly forty years."

"You were good friends, then?"

"Good friends? We were extremely close. I am — I was — also Roger's partner in real estate and especially along the coastal area from Savannah to the Florida line. He owned a number of businesses, as you probably know." Wayne paused to remove his glasses and rub his eyes. He wore an expensive navy pinstriped suit with a vest. Everything about him said either that he had a lot of money or he wanted us to think he did. He was balding and carried a football-sized paunch. "He's — he was — my best friend for more than twenty years. I loved him like — like a brother — perhaps more than a brother."

He took out his handkerchief and wiped his eyes. I stood close enough to see that there were no tears.

"He was my best friend," Wayne said in what was supposed to sound like a blubbery voice.

"Probably *your* only friend," Jason said and stared at him. "Besides that, you weren't *his* friend." Jason was twenty, but as I stared at the peach fuzz on his cheeks, I would have lowered his age by at least three years. Like his mother, Jason had that excellent bone structure and those high cheekbones that would keep him looking young long after he had said good-bye to middle life.

"That was absolutely uncalled for!" Holmestead said loudly. He stared at the boy and pulled his vest down over his paunch. "You have no right to talk to me like that."

"I do when I know what I'm saying. You hated him."

"Look who says such words," Wayne said. "I wonder if I could count the times I heard you scream, 'I hate you! I hate you!' and now you try to accuse me of not —"

"I know what I know!"

"Tell us what you know," Burton said. He turned and draped his arm around Jason's shoulder. It was obvious they knew each other well.

"I heard him just before teatime. I wanted to talk to Dad — and yeah, we had problems in the past." He stared at Burton. "You know about —"

"Yes, I know."

"But — but he and I — well, we got everything straightened out. Uh, well, sort of." He smiled at Burton. "You were the biggest reason — and I guess that's why Dad wanted you to be here tonight. He wanted to thank you. At least, I assume that's why."

"It seems rather easy for you to talk like that, Jason," Wayne said, "but I know he planned to cut you out of his will. You would receive absolutely nothing. Not a penny." He lifted his chin as if to say, "See, I've bested you on that."

"That was true three weeks ago, but we got our differences straightened out," Jason said. "Besides, that's got nothing to do with me. I heard how you talked to him and I heard the names you called him —"

"How dare you attempt to sully my name

with such —"

Burton put up his hand. "Let Jason tell us what he knows, and then you can speak."

"I was outside Dad's office door, and Mr. Holmestead said, 'You're a despicable tyrant. Everyone thinks you're a man of compassion. You can't do this to me! You can't!' That's when Dad looked up, saw me, and said we'd talk after dinner. So I left."

"I said no such thing!"

"Sure you did. You also swore at him — words my mother doesn't want me to use."

"You have a powerful imagination."

"Then ask Simon. He stood at the hall closet. He was supposed to be adding clothes hangers and making space, but he listened. I know he did."

Everyone turned and stared at Simon, who had moved toward the back of the group.

He shrugged. "Maybe."

"Let's get back to the timing," I interrupted. "Can't we narrow this down? Wayne, you saw him at seven o'clock, you say. How did you know it was seven?"

"The evening news had barely started. I spotted Roger on the steps and started to talk to him, but he waved me away, went into his office, and closed the door."

"I saw Wayne when he entered the room,"

said Paulette White, the woman dressed in black.

"Yes, I saw them at the door as I started to descend the staircase." We had to stop then and listen to the speaker tell us all about himself. Dr. Jeffery Mark Dunn taught biology and other first-year science courses at Clayton University on Atlanta's Southside. I knew who he was. In fact, years ago I had signed up for one of his courses, but he was so boring and monotoned, I knew I'd never stay awake.

I dropped the class after the first day. He still wore the same cheap toupee. It was solid black, and the hair that stuck out below was gray. His glasses were now a little thicker, but the voice hadn't changed. He was tall and extremely thin — I guessed about six four — with sharp, bony features. He looked even skinnier than he had when I tried his class eight years earlier.

I probably ought to thank Dr. Dunn. Until I sampled his class, I had planned to go into medicine. He was the major reason I changed my mind. I'm now a psychologist. I've received my doctoral degree from Georgia State, and I'm in private practice.

For the next half hour, Burton made everyone sit down and tell us what he or she was doing before coming to the table.

Just as we started the informal interrogation, Jason said he was hungry, but Mrs. Wright refused to serve anyone. "I am far too upset to think about food. It is in the kitchen. You may help yourself if you choose." She stared down Amanda's stern gaze. "I cannot — I cannot." Crying, she sat down in a corner of the room.

Most of them said they didn't want anything to eat. I think they lied because they assumed that it was the right thing to say. Roger, the man they all claimed to love, had just been murdered. As I gazed around the room, I figured that most of them would move toward the kitchen within minutes.

One by one we all sat down at the table. Lenny, the short, slightly rotund, carrot-headed man, pulled his chair back against the wall and balanced it on two legs.

"Do not do that," Mrs. Wright said with no sign that she'd been crying.

"Okeydokey," he said and grinned. "You're the boss."

"I am *not* the boss. I am merely an employee."

"Is there a Mr. Wright?"

"When was the last time a woman dumped you?" she asked.

"That's irrelevant," he said.

"You are exactly right," she said and

turned her back to him.

Lenny Goss stared at her before his face lit up. "Hey, that's great. You're a great comedian — straight face and all! You rock, mama!" He roared with laughter and turned to me. "Isn't she a hoot?"

"If you say so," I said and tried to give him enough of a smile that he didn't feel offended but not enough that he'd keep talking.

Lenny had enough sense to shut up. He pulled a toothpick out of his jacket pocket and started to pick his teeth. He was about five feet five with elevated heels that brought him to about five seven. He was chubby — that's the kindest word I can use — not quite obese, but he was well on his way. He had that awful carrot-red hair, pale green eyes, and skin pocked with acne scars from his teen years.

"Please eat," Amanda said. She sat at the table twisting a gold lace handkerchief that matched her outfit. As I watched her hands, I sensed that she tried to project a stronger image of the grieving widow than she felt.

It also struck me that no one had walked over to her to express sympathy. Jason was seated next to her and patted her hand a few times. I wasn't sure about his emotions. He had been volatile toward Wayne Holmestead, but now he seemed sad. Was that genuine? I wasn't sure.

"I'm hungry," I said. I got up and walked toward the kitchen. My action seemed to give permission to the others. Jason followed me, and immediately behind him was Reginald Ford. I had met him once — briefly — at Roger's house. If I remember correctly, he is the head of the largest construction firm along the Georgia coast.

He wasn't a particularly good-looking man, but he wasn't ugly. About six feet tall. His prematurely white hair probably made him look older, but as I studied his face, I pegged him for mid- to late thirties. Reginald had an athletic build and wore a tailored shirt that emphasized his muscular arms. But there was something about him I didn't like. I've learned to rely on my instincts, and I felt he wasn't a man I could trust.

Next to him stood the bottled-blond with what I call a plastic smile. Maybe I think of her that way because she was so beautiful. She was probably one of those girls who never had to squeeze a pimple in her life. She wore thin, spiked Charles Jourdan shoes that made her nearly three inches taller than Reginald. She carried a sleek, cornflower blue Hermes shoulder bag that looked perfect with her Chanel suit. Her pale blue scarf probably cost her more than my entire wardrobe.

"Your face looks slightly familiar," I said, "but I don't think we've met."

"Everybody knows me," she said and flashed her plastic smile. She posed with her right arm in the air as though she held a pointer in her hand.

"The weather girl! Beth Wilson! That's who you are!" Lenny said.

"Yes, of course," she said, twirled, and bowed slightly — just the way she performed at the end of each of her weathercasts. She had one of those naturally thin bodies most of us women hate because we know we can't be like her.

"Then you'll want something to eat," I said, unaware of my non sequitur until the words popped out of my mouth. Embarrassed, I turned and led the line back to the kitchen. I'm fairly thin — not Beth Wilson thin — yet when I get nervous, eating calms me down. After all, someone had just been killed. Or maybe I just use that as an excuse. Besides, I know that Mrs. Wright's squid tastes like no one else on the planet can cook it. Okay, Roger insisted we call it calamari, but it's still squid to me.

Eventually we all sat down at the dining

room table. The calamari was excellent, and the vegetables tasted as if they had been cooked at a five-star hotel. The now-lukewarm fish consommé still rated better than at any restaurant I've visited. Amanda didn't appear to have moved from her chair. Lenny had finished his soup, returned to the kitchen, and come back to the table with two bowls for himself.

"You really like that consommé, do you?" I asked.

Lenny had been so busy shoveling it into his mouth, it took two seconds for the message to get through.

"Yeah! Great soup," he said. "It's a little fishy, but great."

"It's supposed to have a fish flavor," Reginald said, "but how would you know the difference?"

Lenny didn't respond but finished off the first bowl, shoved it aside, and spooned out the second. I assumed he could have been eating canned tomato soup and would have said, "Great soup."

Burton had stayed in the dining room. He picked up a glass of water from his place, but he didn't sit down. He moved around as if he were Hercule Poirot or maybe a better dressed and more graceful Columbo.

Without going through a lot of who-cares

details about who said what, it came down to this. Except for Burton and me, everyone else had arrived in time for tea that began promptly at 5:00. He and I had been invited for tea — an English high tea, complete with cucumber sandwiches — but both of us had sent our regrets. I had to see a patient at 2:00, and I couldn't have made the trip from Atlanta in less than four hours. I don't remember why Burton couldn't get there in time.

Everyone agreed they all took tea in the "drawing room" (a term that seems a bit pretentious to me), and Roger left them about 6:25, as far as anyone could remember. He went up to change clothes — something he always did. He had come to tea dressed informally — slacks, loafers, and polo shirt. For dinner, he always put on a dark business suit. He was wearing a pin-striped, dark gray suit when we found his body.

They all had alibis to account for their whereabouts and thus prove their innocence.

My instincts shouted, *They're lying.*

I never doubted my intuition.

In the next few hours, I learned that my instincts had been correct.

3

All the guests claimed to have gone upstairs a few minutes after Roger left them. Simon said that when he picked up the last of the tea dishes at 6:50, no one was in the dining room or the drawing room. He had helped Mrs. Wright set the table.

Beth Wilson said she was the first one to come downstairs, and when she did, she turned on the TV. She wanted to see how well her substitute did. "It was a man," she said in a disgusted tone. She said it was about ten minutes to seven, because she endured the last portion of the dull local news and three minutes before the weather.

"Wayne and I came in immediately behind Beth," Paulette said. "We met at the top of the stairs and came down together."

Jason and his mother were the last ones. They said they had been together in Jason's room.

No one heard anything unusual.

Except for Jason and Amanda, who arrived about 7:20, the other guests claimed to have been in the drawing room from 7:00 until 7:30 for the evening news on CBS. Reginald remembered Beth's weather commentary. Beth had pointed out all the wrong moves made by her substitute — a man with the beginning of male-pattern baldness, which she verbalized three times. "I taught him — or tried to — but he's simply not very good at it."

At 7:30 Wayne Holmestead had turned the TV to CNN and they had watched *Headline News* until a few minutes before eight when they headed into the dining room.

"Why the TV in the drawing room?" Burton asked. "Didn't any of you watch TV in your rooms?"

"TV here only," Simon said as he came back into the dining room.

Burton arched a brow. "One TV set for a house this large?"

"It's the only place where we can get decent reception," Amanda said. "Roger has arranged for a satellite system hookup or whatever they call it, but it won't be in effect for another couple of weeks."

"Still no phone service?" Burton asked Simon.

Simon shook his head.

"Could someone have cut the phone lines?"

He shook his head a second time. "Checked."

"We have only two phones in this house," Amanda said. "One is in Roger's office, and the other is in the kitchen."

"Couldn't you have installed more?" I asked.

"Roger liked it that way," she said and looked away.

That seemed odd to me. The flicker in Burton's eyes said he agreed.

"We have had trouble with the telephone most of the week," Mrs. Wright said. She shrugged, probably an unconscious imitation of Simon. "We are used to it. If the phone works, we use it. If it does not, we wait for one or two days."

Something about Mrs. Wright seemed odd. Her language carried a stiffness to it. I decided to watch her more closely, although I'm not certain why.

"Stay from office," said Simon as if we hadn't remembered. "Locked until police." He held up a key and then put it inside his pants pocket. I assumed that was the only key.

"Good idea," I said, and several others

nodded. I couldn't think of a reason why anyone would want to go into a room containing a dead body.

Wayne Holmestead insisted he had spent most of the newscast time writing e-mails on his BlackBerry, even though he hadn't been able to send them. He held out his BlackBerry for Burton to examine.

I liked the way Burton went around the room. His manner was so gentle that no one seemed to feel he interrogated them. I wondered why he had wasted his time to become a minister. He would have made an excellent therapist. I would have hired him, and I'm a good judge of people.

"This must be difficult for you," Burton said and made direct eye contact with Amanda. "If you want to talk about it now, it might make it easier for you later on when the police come."

Tears glistened in her eyes, and she brushed them away with her hand. She wore clear nail polish, and it looked perfect on her. I wished I were as graceful or had beautiful hands like hers.

"Jason and I came downstairs. The news had been on perhaps ten minutes, but it might have been longer. I sat in the chair at the far side of the room and stayed there until Mrs. Wright announced it was time for dinner."

"That's right, and I sat next to her," Jason said. "Just like I'm sitting next to her right now. So that means neither of us could have hurt Dad."

"Or both of you did it," Beth said. Then she smiled.

"How dare you say that!" Jason said. "That was totally out of line."

"Of course. You're right. I apologize." The smile pattern was so firmly in place that it seemed to me as if she couldn't talk without the smile. That's always something serious to watch. No normal person smiles all the time.

Each of the guests claimed to have been in the drawing room. It was a high-ceilinged room about forty by thirty feet with no windows. The house was amazingly large, with ten bedrooms on the second floor and five on the third. Roger had it decorated with commissioned paintings and busts from artists he liked. I liked the paintings but didn't think much of the sculptures. They might have been artistic masterpieces, but they all had a kind of sameness to them. Their drabness didn't do anything to accentuate the rosewood rococo furniture.

While Burton asked routine questions, I gazed at the paintings on the walls. I don't know anything about art, but these particular pieces had a cold gloominess about them. For example, I recognized the lighthouse at St. Simon's Island — which was located less than twenty miles away. The artist painted it at dusk with fog moving in, and I could see a tiny light at the top. Aside from the light, the colors ran from light gray to black.

"And no one left the room until after Mrs. Wright called you to dinner. Is that correct?"

"Oh, but yes, I did get up at one time," Tonya Borders said. "Just once."

Tonya spoke with a slight Slavic accent — at least most of the time. I have a fairly good ear for accents, and she confused me. Sometimes she sounded like she was from Eastern Europe or Russia and at other times like she was from the Deep South. That accent made me decide to watch her more carefully. She tried to smile but wasn't very good at it and could have taken lessons from Weather Girl.

She patted her silvery-brown bun and smoothed out her hair. "I, uh, went to the little girls' room." She leaned forward as if she wanted Burton to have her undivided attention. "A commercial had just begun, and the news was just coming back on when

I returned."

Why, that old prune is flirting with Burton, I thought.

"So that gave you a good two minutes," Paulette said. "And it would have been so easy for you to make a detour to Roger's office." She turned to Burton and said, "She would have had to walk past his office to get to the only restroom on this floor."

"Yes, I did pass his office," Tonya said, "but I must assure you that I did not stop and shoot him on the way. I loved Roger. I truly loved that gentleman." The Slavic accent was really thick. "I owe him so much for my career and have always had such deep personal feelings for him." She made another attempt to smile at Burton after she spoke the last words.

"Yes, dear, we all loved Roger," Amanda said to Tonya in a tone that wasn't quite convincing. She leaned over and patted Tonya's hand. "And, Burton, although I realize someone here killed my husband, I find it nearly impossible to believe that any of the people in this room would want to hurt him. These were his friends. They all loved him — at least as far as I know — and he had helped each one of them. They weren't just his friends, but close friends."

"I wasn't a close friend," I blurted out.

"Yes, but he had deep regard for you. Very deep," Wayne said. "He told me so."

"Really?" I asked.

"I would never hurt him in any way, let alone kill him," Tonya said. "Death is, well, so . . . so final. And so very, very sad." Now her voice sounded like an imitation of Katharine Hepburn with a Slavic accent.

"I also left the room once," Jeffery Dunn said. "My doctor has me on a prescription antibiotic, and I take one with each meal. I had forgotten to bring down a pill, so I went upstairs." He turned to Amanda. "I walked right past you."

"Perhaps you did," she said. "I honestly don't remember. My mind was on the news."

"Yes, I remember seeing the good Dr. Dunn get up," Wayne Holmestead said.

"How long was he gone?" I asked.

"I'm not sure. It did seem like several minutes, maybe as long as ten minutes."

"It was nine minutes. You see, I could not find my medication. I had to search through my luggage."

"Did you find it?" I asked.

"Yes, I did." He went into a lengthy and boring-as-usual explanation that he couldn't find the medicine but remembered having packed it. He took us through every step of

47

his search through his luggage. He explained that he always made a list of everything he needed for the trip and had checked every item to indicate that it was inside one of his two suitcases. His antibiotic was the seventeenth item on the list. So he knew he had to search until he found it. He found the pills finally, because the container, which was only one inch high and three inches long and made of clear plastic, had slipped inside one of his folded shirts. He also unpacked everything while he was there. "I was gone exactly nine minutes. I have a habit of timing myself when I do things like that."

"Very thorough," Burton said, and I wondered if that was sarcasm in his voice. Probably not from him.

I had listened to everyone talk, but something bothered me. Perhaps it was the therapist part of me at work. I turned to Weather Girl, the smile lady. "Did you like Roger — I mean really like him?"

"Didn't I say I did?" She did her facial thing before she added, "I adored him, simply, simply adored him. He was so much older, of course, so there was no romantic involvement." She paused, and another plastic smile filled her face before she spoke again. "I assure you, I owed him so much.

He was, uh, like a dear uncle or an older brother." This time she smiled at Burton.

Doesn't he get it? That yucky every-second smile — she's such a phony, I thought. Maybe Burton isn't as sharp as I thought he was.

I turned to Jeffery and asked, "Did you like Roger?"

"Like him? What a strange and positively absurd question. I was his guest, his friend, and he was someone I'd known and liked," he said. "We'd been close for many years." He started to explain how they had met and where, but Burton interrupted and thanked him.

I winked at Burton for doing that. Had Jeffery been allowed to continue, I'm sure we would have had to hear what he ate for lunch the day the two men met, and he may even have taken us on an endless journey back to his childhood days.

Burton's eyes caught mine and locked for perhaps one second. I was sure he sensed what I was feeling. Maybe he did catch on to Beth's one facial expression.

"Hey, I'm the most unlikely one to have shot old Rog," Lenny said, "but that would probably make me the most likely suspect."

He laughed at his little joke. Or what I assumed was a joke.

"Really! I meant that. Don't you people watch TV? It's always the one —"

"You never left the room?" I asked.

"Hey, babe, exactly right," he said and winked, "but I would have left the room with you anytime!"

"You are rather crude, you know," Reginald Ford said. Before Lenny answered, he looked at me. "I apologize for him. He's not my friend, merely an acquaintance. We rode together from the mainland, and he assumes we are now chums or buddies or at least that I like him. I assure you he's equally offensive to everyone."

Lenny burst out laughing. "I love this guy. What a sense of humor. He absolutely kills me." As he heard his own last words, he had enough sensitivity to blush and mumble, "Sorry."

"But to answer your question before you ask," Reginald said, "I did not leave the room. Neither did Lenny, so I can vouch for him. I tried to watch the news, and his mouth ran the whole time."

"Hey, Reggie boy, are you trying to insult me or something?" Lenny yelled and laughed.

"I gave up trying. You're immune." He cleared his throat and said, "I am not Reggie and I am not Reg. My name is Reginald. Please — for at least the tenth time."

Lenny laughed again. "You got it, Reggie boy! From now on it's only Reginald."

Reginald raised his hands in defeat. He got up from the table, took his chair, and moved to the end farthest from Lenny.

"Why don't I pour everyone a glass of sweet tea?" Amanda said and got up. Her hands were shaking. She tried to pick up the tall pitcher in front of her but couldn't seem to coordinate. "Jason, come and help me."

As soon as Burton looked at me again, I motioned my head toward the door. He caught on immediately, and we both left. So that no one would overhear us, I didn't say a word until after I led him outside the house and we stood on the antebellum-style porch. It had four large columns that were probably supposed to look as if it had come from *Gone with the Wind.* The porch encircled the entire front of the house.

Storm clouds flooded the sky, and within seconds they had hidden the moon. The heavens became black and forbidding. The wind felt damp; rain was certainly on its way.

"Everyone keeps saying how much he or she loved Roger," I said.

"It doesn't ring true, does it?"

"That's exactly the way I felt. What do you think is going on?"

"You're the therapist," Burton said.

"And that weather girl —" Okay, that was catty of me, but the words came out anyway.

Burton laughed.

"Why are you laughing?"

"Why are you jealous of her?" he asked. "She's as self-closed as you are open."

I smiled — no, I grinned. I had to revise my opinion of him once again. This man was really bright.

The first raindrops landed softly on the window next to me. Enough light came through from the hallway that I could see his warm smile. I felt it was genuine — the first truly genuine smile I had seen since coming into the house.

"You're leading this investigation," I said, "so you tell me."

"They're lying. I mean, really lying," he said. "They loathed Roger."

"That's a bit strong —"

"Yes, but it's true —"

"I absolutely agree," I said, "but I wonder why. Why would they hate him? If they hated him, why would they come here? Roger hasn't made it easy to visit — being on an island."

"Why did *you* dislike him? If I could

52

understand that, maybe I could understand why the others didn't like him."

His words shocked me. I thought I had covered my feelings well. After all, I'm a therapist, and we're careful to remain objective and not to show our emotions. I wonder how he had discerned that I didn't like Roger.

"What do you mean?" I asked trying to equivocate while I figured out how to answer.

Burton wouldn't play my game; he waited for me to respond.

"I didn't want to see him dead. It wasn't that kind of dislike."

"What kind of dislike was it?"

"My dislike had nothing to do with his death or with any of the others. It was, uh, a personal thing with Roger."

"Do you think his murder was impersonal?"

This man was good. Maybe he should have been on the police force. "Of course, it was personal," I said. Burton had started to move in a direction I didn't want him to go. "I didn't kill him — *as you know.* My feelings were — well, something I choose not to discuss. Because you know I'm innocent, I'm sure you won't push me."

"That's an excellent answer, and you've

also set the limits on how far I can go with you," he said, and I saw his dimples up close. He could pose for a toothpaste ad on TV.

"Good," I said.

"However, just this — you're sure it has nothing to do with his death? Really sure?"

"Positive."

And I was sure.

At least I was then.

4

Before Burton and I went back inside the house, we agreed on a strategy. He would ask questions, and I would listen. He laughed and added, "You know that's what we preachers do — we talk — and you therapists listen."

Frankly, that juvenile attempt at humor didn't deserve a smile, but I gave him one anyway because I liked the man. "I reserve the right to change my mind or to interrupt."

He shrugged exactly like Simon, so perfectly it was as if he had taken lessons. Then I really smiled.

"Would you like to reverse roles?" he asked.

"I'll let you know if you're not doing an adequate job," I said. Okay, I gave him a third smile, and this time it was to deflect any offense my smart remark may have caused.

His face showed me that he hadn't been offended. I liked this guy even better. He could be direct, but he wasn't offensive or defensive. He didn't have that fragile male ego that jumped at every careless word. I wish he had been one of my blind dates instead of some of those vain, self-centered, over-the-hill jocks I had dated.

Back inside the drawing room, Burton asked everyone to sit down. Three people came from the dining room with plates of food. Lenny had his plate so full I hoped he could balance everything until he sat down. No matter how fancy the meal, Roger always had Mrs. Wright cook a few Southern dishes, such as collard greens. Half of one plate contained the watery greens. I've been in the South all my life, but collard greens are far from my favorite food, and I hate the smell. I was glad I wasn't near Lenny.

Lenny sat on a straight-backed chair — as straight as those rococo chairs can be — and dug away without dropping a single pea or a tiny shard of lettuce. To his credit, he didn't drip any of the vinegar water from the collards. I'll say this for him — he sure knew how to handle his food.

I thought it was odd that not everyone ate in the dining room, but now they came into the drawing room with mounds of food on their plates — even those who had already eaten. Roger never would have allowed them to do that. I wondered if that was the reason they did so now.

They joined the others who sat and ate casually. Everyone seemed to have dropped the pretense. No one any longer made a show of being overcome by grief.

I looked around and counted. We were eleven people. Everyone was in the room except Simon Presswood and Elaine Wright.

I watched the way they ate. Dr. Dunn attacked his food as if it would run away from him. Wayne took dainty bites as if large ones would be too much to chew. Tonya Borders sat quite still, bent slightly forward as if she would repel anyone who tried to taste her food. Paulette White had a plate half filled with food, but she had made no attempt to eat anything. Reginald Ford was the only one who seemed to eat normally.

It still seemed bizarre to me. Other than Jason and Amanda, they seemed untouched by the death of the man they all claimed to have loved. Occasionally, Amanda shed a few tears and Jason wrapped his arm around her to comfort her. He spoke softly, and I couldn't hear what he said.

"Thank you, dear," she murmured several times.

I was sure Burton would want to stop and get himself something to eat, but he didn't. In fact, I'm not sure he ate all night. I had eaten plenty, but I went back to the kitchen for a large bowl of ambrosia — another dream from our superb cook. She used fruit and coconut, but she added some special ingredient that made me realize why my grandmother used to call it the food of the Greek gods.

Even though I ate an immense amount of ambrosia, it still wasn't enough. Gnawing hunger pains — or what I perceived as hunger pains — grabbed at my stomach. I had an energy bar in my pocket. I pulled it out and nibbled on it. I thought of going to the kitchen for more food, but I didn't want to miss out on anything, and who knows what might happen while I was out of the room. I felt my other pocket and found three pieces of peppermint candy. I would be fine.

Just then, Tonya Borders put her plate on the table. She took off her glasses and put her head in her hands. I sensed she posed as a picture of grief more than she felt the emotion. Of course, Burton was directly in front of her, and I suspected she made the gesture for his benefit. She didn't go into the grief act until Burton looked her way.

As I watched, I thought, *Honey, I doubt you ever feel any true emotion.*

Burton waited until she finished her melodramatic pose and had summoned a tear or two. She held a handkerchief in her right hand and gently wiped her eyes.

"As each of you has talked about where you were and your relationship to Roger," Burton said, and his gaze moved from face to face, "you made a point of saying how much you loved Roger."

"And of course we did, and I certainly do, and I'll say it as often as you wish to hear the words," Wayne spoke up. "He was my dearest friend, my closest associate, and —"

"Excellent. Suppose we start with you. Tell us about your relationship with Roger."

Burton's soft voice and smile would put anyone at ease. *Burton, old boy, you are amazing,* I thought. *You make it clear what you want, but there's something about the way you interact so that people don't feel offended or intimidated.*

"To begin with," Wayne said and paused to clear his throat. "I owed that wonderful man so much for his help through the years. In fact, many, many people owed Roger a great deal, you know, especially here in Glynn County."

"And why is that?" I asked.

59

"I'll tell you," Beth interrupted. "More than anyone else, Roger has given so much to so many." She sounded as if she were reading from a prompter. "For example, he invested millions to improve the coastal area and it has attracted more than twenty new businesses in the past two years."

"That's correct," Wayne said. "Another example is tourism. Because of his endeavors, tourism is on the rise by nearly 30 percent this year. He planned to bring in a regional opera company to attract tourists from November until March."

Whenever Wayne spoke, he pulled down on his vest. Maybe he thought it would hide his paunch. Although I had observed Wayne do that before, I now realized that was one of his frequent mannerisms.

"In what way did he help business? What did he do?" Burton asked. As I watched, I knew he didn't care about the answer. He simply wanted to keep Wayne Holmestead talking.

"For one thing, he brought in a fish-canning factory. The experts said it couldn't be done and there wouldn't be enough business —"

"But he proved them wrong," Paulette said. "That was typical of his brilliance. And he was brilliant, you know. He made that factory profitable within the first year." She dabbed her mouth gently with her napkin. "In case you are unaware, that was quite a financial achievement for such a short span of time."

"That's not all," Wayne said. "If you go down to the beach along the coast — anywhere south of Savannah — you'll be amazed at how pristine the beaches are. He cleaned them up — every inch — and paid for everything himself. Jekyll Island and St. Simon's Island used to get all the tourists because the beaches around Brunswick were dirty. The odor of dead fish repelled people."

"He was very shrewd, you know," Beth Wilson said.

"Beth is right," Wayne said. "He had that uncanny sense of what would work. People had stopped visiting here more than thirty years ago. Roger changed that mind-set." He paused and licked his lips, and it was obvious to me that this was also part of a well-rehearsed presentation. "There is also the matter of the —"

"And you have been part of those projects, haven't you?" Burton asked. He smiled and patted Wayne on the shoulder.

"We were partners in the ventures. We wanted to help others and worked to benefit the people. We wanted unemployment to be less than 1 percent — perhaps that was not possible to achieve, but it was our goal. We cared about —"

"Commendable. That's truly humanitarian," I said with some sarcasm in my voice.

"We believed in serving others." He either hadn't gotten my sarcasm or ignored it.

"Surely you made a few dollars," Burton said. "Even with great humanitarian projects, there must have been opportunities for financial reward."

Good old Burton. He knows how to do it. I began to wonder if we were going to play good cop, bad cop.

"Oh, well, of course, I've, uh, made money — not a great deal — but uh, I made money on my investments. That's one incentive, but —"

"He means he's made a fortune, a very, very big fortune, by buying property along the coast," Jason said. "As soon as he knew Dad was going to clean up the beaches, he bought everything he could, held them until after the cleanup, and resold them at exorbitant prices —"

"That is not entirely accurate," Wayne said. "I did buy property. Any astute businessman would. I — uh, had started to buy before —"

"Stop lying!" Jason said. "That was part

of what Dad got angry about. He had just learned that you bought all those properties near the ocean through some offshore corporation. You took advantage of local people until after —"

"You were obviously eavesdropping. You nasty —"

"Yeah, I was." Jason gave him the full-mouth grin. His light brown eyes lit up, and he raised his chin as if to say, "So hit me."

"This — this vile boy grossly exaggerates —"

"Perhaps we can change the tone of this interrogation or whatever it is," Tonya said. "While I want to go on record" — she stared at Burton and then at me — "that is, if there is a record, I loved Roger. He trusted me and opened many doors of opportunity for my career. It would have been stupid of me to want to get rid of him." She paused as if to make certain we understood. "I've been one of Roger's lawyers — his most trusted lawyer — for nearly twenty years." Her Slavic accent had disappeared somewhere after she said she wanted to go on record.

I leaned forward, looked directly at Tonya, and said, "I think you wanted to tell us something before you launched into the matter of your close relationship with Roger."

Her stare might have frozen an adversary in litigation proceedings, but she didn't intimidate me.

"Uh, yes, I suppose you are correct." She glared at me and took a deep breath. "All right, I shall tell you the truth: I came because I had no choice." Her accent was extremely noticeable again. "I received a *summons* to attend."

"That is being a bit harsh," Jeffery Dunn said. "I will not have my good friend's reputation besmirched —"

"You are a hypocrite," she said softly, but her dark eyes expressed her venom. "Yes, it was an invitation — a *written* invitation, mind you — something I had never received in all my years of dealing with Roger, but still —"

"We all received such an *invitation*." Jeffery overcame his monotone to emphasize the last word.

"You are too much, Jeffery. I am quite certain Dr. Burton will discover the truth, so we might as well speak up." Tonya actually batted her eyes twice as she looked at Burton. "I shall then say it more plainly. I have worked for Roger for many years — as I have already stated. He did a great deal for my career, and I assume that's true of the others. But through all those years, he treated us like indentured servants. I observed that he treated Simon and Elaine better than he did us."

"That information surprises me," Burton said, "although I scarcely knew him."

"It's true," Amanda said. Jason had brought her a plate, although she had not eaten more than one or two bites. "He did treat us all rather shabbily."

"So you came because you were afraid of Roger?" I asked. "All of you?"

"Of course they did!" Jason said. "They knew Dad could make them or break them financially. They may have despised him in their hearts, but if Dad had told them to, they would have crawled into the house on their knees."

"You are a rude child," Beth said, but her face expressed nothing but sweetness. Was she some kind of *Stepford Wives* clone?

"That is not exactly true, Jason. There was a reason we came — and just the eleven of us — and no one else," Tonya said. "Roger had an announcement to make. It was something that involved all of us."

"How do you know that?" Amanda asked.

"He added a handwritten note on my *summons*." Tonya glared at Jeffery. "The message said, 'I have something important to tell you and the others.' Just that."

"A summons?" I asked.

Her face hardened. "I would hardly call it anything else. Or perhaps you would prefer the word *demand*."

5

"A summons?" I repeated Tonya's words. "Or a demand?"

"What was the nature of the announcement?" Burton asked.

"I have no idea," she said.

"Roger didn't write warm, sweet notes," Beth said. "So I assumed it was something — something ominous." She said the handwritten note on her invitation read, "I plan to make an important announcement, and I want you here. It affects you."

"You mean you expected some kind of exposure?" I asked.

Without changing a facial muscle, Beth said, "If you choose to say it that way."

"Did the rest of you receive a personal note with your invitation?" Burton asked.

"I thought it was just a big joke," Lenny said and laughed. But his laughter didn't sound genuine.

"Roger never joked about such things,"

Reginald said. "In fact, I don't think our dear, departed Roger ever joked about anything. And yes, I received a handwritten note in which he said he had an important announcement that would affect my life."

"I did, too," I said.

"So did I," Burton said. "It seemed slightly odd to me. You know, I'd met the man only once before. Do any of you know anything more about the announcement?"

One way or another, everyone murmured that they didn't know or said, "Nothing."

"That's strange," I said. "When I received my *invitation*" (and I emphasized that word), "I assumed it had something to do with a personal thing — something Roger and I had spoken about before. Obviously I was mistaken. Mine said he had something *important* to talk to me about, but it didn't sound ominous. Apparently, it was something that affected all of us."

"Yes, strange," said Lenny. "And I thought I was special and that he liked me the most!" He started to laugh, but even he realized it wasn't funny.

"Amanda, what about you?" I asked. "You're his wife, so surely —"

"I don't know." Tears slid down her cheeks. "I had no idea. I didn't get such a note. I mean, I'm his wife and —"

Burton and I momentarily locked eyes. We realized Amanda had almost blurted out something and then censored herself.

"He must have confided something to you, Amanda," Jeffery said.

She shook her head. "Nothing."

"Leave her alone." Jason handed her his white handkerchief, and she wiped her eyes. "Don't you have any respect for her grief?"

"It's all right, dear," she said. "I had no idea because I have not lived in this house for three weeks. Roger and I had a rather nasty row, and I moved to Savannah —"

"That's certainly news to me," Paulette White said. "Dear Roger never said a word to me."

"And it's none of your business, either, because —"

Amanda held out her hand to silence her son. "I had already started divorce proceedings."

Paulette gasped.

"I've never spoken about this to anyone — except to Jason, of course."

"And Roger hadn't been much of a father to me — I mean, most of the time," Jason said and turned to Burton.

"It's okay, son," he said and wrapped his arm around the boy's shoulder.

"I'm ready to talk, and I'd like to talk.

That may help me sort out things." Amanda leaned her head back and closed her eyes. "I might as well start down the line of truth. I want to tell you I had an extremely miserable life with Roger. For years, I've been careful to maintain a charade and mask my unhappiness."

"Yes, it must have been miserable counting all those millions!" Lenny said.

"You really are obnoxious," Reginald said.

Lenny received enough glares that he mumbled, "Sorry," and shut up.

"He exerted a strange kind of control. I had to give him a reason every time I left the island. I had to account for everything I did." She started twisting Jason's handkerchief the way she had her own at the table. "He didn't mind my spending money — he actually encouraged me — and I was allowed to buy whatever I wanted." She paused and opened her eyes. "I wonder if you heard what I just said?"

"Heard every word," Beth said. "Poor rich woman."

"You still don't get it, do you? I'll make myself clearer. Spending his money was never an issue. What made my life so miserable was that I had to inform him first. Roger said *inform*, but he meant ask for permission and explain what I planned to do."

"I'm sure you're just overwrought," Paulette said, "and overstating —"

"No, I'm not." She glared at Paulette. "Did you know that I had to tell him which car I wanted to drive? He bought two cars for my use. We keep both at our private garage at dockside. They were his gift to me, he said, and for my use. *My use.* I was the only one who drove them, *but* —"

"How sad, how very sad for you," Tonya said, and this time she truly sounded like Greta Garbo. "I have seen your severe punishment. Your Aston Martin V12 and your Mercedes-Benz 30082 Roadster. Both of them, I believe, cost more than most people earn in a single year."

"I think you've missed the point, Tonya," I said. "Let Amanda explain."

"Roger did provide those cars. He urged me to buy a Ferrari when I told him I was leaving. He thought material things mattered — as if another car would make me less miserable."

"I get the picture," I said, "but I'm not sure everyone understands."

"It's quite simple. I could have the best of anything, but I had to let him know which one I chose. *Every time.* Worse than that, he provided a palm pad with some kind of mini spreadsheet, and I had to list every place I stopped and jot down the mileage each time. When I left the car, the figures I wrote down had to match the mileage the car showed. I felt like a prisoner."

"Oh, my dear dear Amanda. I had no idea," Wayne said. "I'm sorry —"

"Liar! You knew!" Jason said.

"Do you realize what it's like?" Amanda said, as if she had not been interrupted. "At the end of each month, I had to account for every cent I spent — and I mean to the penny — or he would give me no allowance for the next month."

"I had no idea." Wayne knelt in front of her and patted her hand.

Hmm, I thought, *I wonder if that idiot is trying to nuzzle up to the widow.*

She pushed him away. "You may have been Roger's best friend — I don't know about that — but you are not mine. I don't want your false display of sympathy."

I wanted to shout hoorah for Amanda.

She stood up, turned her back to everyone for perhaps a full minute, and then spun around and faced us. "The rest of you may have loved Roger Harden, but I didn't. Perhaps at one time, in the beginning, I loved him. I'm not even sure now, because there have been so many miserable years since then. I married Roger, as most of you know, after my first husband died and left me with a two-year-old son. Roger's first wife divorced him. Do you know why she left him? She left him because of his constant attempt to control her life."

"He was a bit demanding," Paulette said. "I'll admit that, but —"

"A bit?" Tears raced rapidly down Amanda's cheeks. "I'll say it better then. Roger Harden was a power-hungry, totally controlling monster, and I detested him."

"I'm sorry your life has been that bad, Amanda, but that's the most honest thing anyone has said this evening," I added.

"Then why did you come, Amanda?" Burton asked.

I hadn't thought to ask that question. I was so caught up in genuine sympathy for Amanda. I walked over and draped my arms around her. She was about five inches shorter than I was, and she laid her head against my shoulder and cried.

Burton held up his hand for silence, and no one said anything until Amanda stopped crying. She used Jason's handkerchief to wipe her eyes.

"Why did you come back to the island?" Burton softly asked again.

"He called me. Yesterday."

"True," Simon said. "I heard. Phone."

"He did call, and it was rather strange. He *asked* me to come. It wasn't a summons. He said, 'Will you come? Please.' In eighteen years, Roger had never *asked* me for anything, and I didn't know the word *please* was in his vocabulary. I'm not sure what was going on with him, but I knew it was something significant."

"Did he say why he wanted you here?" I asked.

She shook her head slowly. "I asked — twice — but he was evasive. He said at least three times, 'I have something significant — something I have to tell you and the others. I want to make my announcement once and to all of you at the same time.' That was the most I could get out of him."

"Is there anything else you can tell us?" I asked. "Are you holding back? I don't know why, but I sense that there's something you're not telling us. Is there?"

"Tell them, Mom," Jason said.

"It's not something I can readily explain. It was — it was as if he was different. His voice was softer . . . kinder perhaps. That may not mean anything to the rest of you, but I had lived with him for eighteen years. Just before we hung up, I asked, 'What has

74

happened to you?' "

"And what did he say?"

" 'I've made an important decision, and I want a special group of people here. It affects them.' I asked him about the decision, but he refused to say."

"But you admit you hated him?" Paulette asked.

"Yes. But I came anyway because — well, because I hoped — I truly hoped he had changed for the better. I have prayed for him every day, and on the phone he begged —"

"And, of course, you didn't want him to cut you off financially," Paulette said. "He would have, you know. Roger was capable of such acts."

"You are despicable," Amanda lashed out.

Paulette smiled as if she had won a victory in the courtroom.

"Money? That had nothing to do with Mom's decision," Jason said. "I won't have you talk that way to her."

Amanda held up her hand to silence her son. "That's sweet of you, darling." She faced Paulette and said, "I didn't need Roger's money. I have enough — more than enough without him."

"I doubt that," Lenny said. "No woman ever has enough." He laughed loudly, and everyone ignored him.

"I have money. When my first husband died, I received a large insurance settlement. My parents were well off. They left me enough money that I could have lived comfortably for the rest of my life. So you see, I didn't need Roger's money."

"That's true," Wayne said. "I can vouch for that."

"So what about you, dear Paulette," Beth purred. "Maybe your motive wasn't so pure."

"I can tell all of you this much," Paulette said, "I resented Roger at times, but I didn't hate him."

"Not true," Simon said. "Lie."

We stared at Simon, but he would say nothing more.

"If you know something, please tell us," I pleaded.

"Truth will come," he said. He took his plate of half-eaten food and returned to the kitchen.

I got up and started to go after him, but Burton shook his head. I gave him a splendid Simon shrug and sat down.

"Is there a gun in the house?" Burton asked. "I don't know why I didn't ask earlier."

"Yes, Mr. Harden kept a gun in his office.

It's in the bottom drawer of his desk, and he keeps the drawer unlocked." Elaine Wright said to Burton, "Follow me and I'll show you."

"I think the rest of us should stay here," I said.

Wayne Holmestead immediately attacked his food again as if he hadn't eaten in days. Tonya stared into space and sipped whatever was in her cup.

Within a minute, Burton and Mrs. Wright returned. Before he spoke, I could tell from the expression on his face what he was going to say.

"The gun is gone."

6

"Whoever shot poor Roger must have stolen the gun," Reginald said and then blushed. "I suppose that's obvious, isn't it?"

Lenny opened his mouth, but this time he had enough sense to close it in silence.

For several minutes, we discussed the possibility of searching every room to find the missing gun — which we assumed was the weapon that had killed Roger — but it was a large house, and the hiding-place possibilities were endless.

Mrs. Wright went to try the telephone. She came back to say it was still out. "Perhaps by morning we shall have service again," she said.

"I don't know about anyone else, but I intend to go to my room," Jeffery said. "I have several important lectures that I plan to give as a guest speaker next month, and I need to prepare." He turned and left us.

I had to stuff my hand in my mouth not

to burst out laughing. He taught the basic biology course and three other basic science courses. Everyone at the university knew he hadn't changed a word in his lectures in years — whether in the classroom or as a guest at an outside venue. I had no idea what he needed to do, but it wasn't to prepare lectures.

"I am too upset to serve anyone or to wash the dishes," Mrs. Wright said. "The kitchen is open. Do what you want." She started for the door, paused, and looked back. "I did not hate Mr. Harden, and I cannot stand to listen to the rest of you lie about how you feel."

"Did you love him?" Burton asked.

"I did not. Furthermore, he did not treat me well, but I — I owed him a debt. He promised me that I would have the debt paid by the end of this year."

"What kind of debt?" Burton asked.

"That, sir, is none of your business. I did not hate him. I did not and would not kill him. There are people in this room who had reasons to kill him, but I am not one of them."

"Please explain, would you?" Burton said.

Her gaze shifted across the room, and then she stared at her feet. "Those who have things to hide know who they are. I have nothing to hide. I know what I have seen with my own eyes." She left the drawing room.

I didn't understand what was going on. I heard her words, but I sensed she was giving someone some kind of message. A warning perhaps?

Burton looked my way. It was uncanny, but I knew he had picked up the same vibration.

One by one the others left the room. Jason and Amanda sat in a corner and whispered to one another for several minutes. At one point, Jason put his arm around her shoulder. "Let's go upstairs," he said. Without waiting for a response, he led his mother from the room.

Soon everyone was gone except Burton and me.

If Burton's eyes said what I thought they did, he had caught everything. In fact, he may have been ahead of me.

"What do you think?" he asked me.

I started to do the Simon shrug and stopped. "What do *you* think?"

"Two things. First, Mrs. Wright was intentionally being cryptic, and I have no idea why. I knew it would do no good to push."

"I agree. And the second?"

"Rather obvious, I suppose, but Amanda

isn't the only person who didn't love Roger. In fact, no one at the table tonight even liked him. Jason used to hate him — I can safely tell you that much. I have no idea what's accounted for the change, but his hatred is gone."

"What about Simon? We know he didn't kill Roger. At least if he did, he had to do it before he made his final trip to pick us up. Is that possible?"

"I hadn't thought of that," Burton said.

Just then Simon walked into the dining room. He quietly picked up the dirty dishes.

"I have a question for you," Burton said to him. "You were on the dock to meet us, but you didn't arrive until ten minutes after seven and —"

"Good logic, but not kill."

"Did anyone see you?" I asked.

He nodded. "Four trips first." He held up his fingers. "Put on different pants. Served tea. Never alone. Talked to Mr. Goss five minutes before seven. Follow me to dock." He shook his head. "That man. Many words. I wait mainland from 7:04."

"You're amazing, Simon," I said. "You use the minimum number of words, but I always figure out what you mean."

As I expected, he shrugged. But he did something else. Before he turned to leave, he winked at me. This time I didn't know what he meant.

"That eliminates him," Burton said. "Agreed?"

Burton hadn't seen the wink, and I didn't think that was the time to discuss it. Besides, I had something else I wanted to ask. "Why did you get an invitation?" I asked. "You don't seem to fit with these people."

"I assume it was because of Jason. At least that's the primary reason I came. He was quite a troubled teen when we met. He was a student at Clayton U. He and some of his classmates played basketball in our church gym, and we got to know each other. After a few weeks, he asked to talk to me. We met regularly, and he got better."

"He was troubled? In what way?"

He gave me that handsome-hunk grin, but he didn't say a word.

"Okay," I said. "It was worth a try to ask. It was a good test to see if you ministers talked about your parishioners."

"I can't speak for all ministers. I can, however, speak for myself."

"You just did. You're good. You know that?"

He shrugged. "See, I can imitate Simon, too." Then he turned on that fabulous smile before he asked, "So why did you get an invitation?"

"As you probably know, Roger lived in Clayton County for a number of years. He was a kind of benefactor to me."

"Kind of?"

"I'm a therapist. At the time, I hadn't finished my doctoral program and did only private counseling. Roger intervened, and I became the head of Clayton County Special Services."

"Intervened? How did he do that?"

"The way he influences most people in the state." I laughed, but Burton didn't get it. "Okay, his influence is called money. He gives money, lots and lots of money, to the right causes and at the right time —"

"The causes where he can be in control?"

"Something like that. But I honestly thought my record and my work had gained me the position. It might have anyway. As Roger put it, he was my insurance."

A peal of thunder punctuated my last few words. It reverberated in the window glass. The rainstorm was on the way.

"This is unusual — the weather I mean," I said. "This is June. It's too early for this kind of storm."

Blasts of thunder rolled like great broken wheels of stone across the sky. A strong, gusty wind pummeled the roof.

Burton seemed hardly aware of the weather or my comment. He stared into space for a long time before he said, "I'm not sure where to go next, and you obviously don't want to go down the path we've started. One thing bothers me about those last words of Mrs. Wright. I have a niggling feeling —"

"That she knows more than she's willing to tell? Or that maybe she meant her words as a message to someone?"

"Exactly that. You sensed it, too? I felt as if she answered me but was talking to someone else."

"Let's go find her," I said.

We walked into the dining room, which was empty, and into the kitchen, but she wasn't there, either. Simon sat at the kitchen table with his back to us. In front of him was a steaming cup of tea with the string of the bag hanging over the side.

When I asked Simon which room was hers, he used his chin to point toward the kitchen door, "Number one."

That seemed like an odd response, or it would have if it had come from someone else. We went through the door and walked down the hall. The first room had the number one on it. Burton and I looked at each other and smiled, and I said, "Elementary, my dear Dr. Watson."

Burton knocked, but no one answered. He knocked a second time and leaned close to the door to detect movement inside. He shook his head and turned to walk away.

"Let me knock," I said. I knocked with one hand, and with the other I turned the knob. Her door opened. I walked inside and turned on the light, and it was obvious she wasn't there. I had assumed Number one meant a tiny room, but it was a small apartment. I stood in what resembled a den, complete with a sofa and an easy chair. The furniture certainly didn't match the rest of the house. This looked as if it had come from Sears — sturdy, usable, but not expensive.

She had her own kitchen — which I could see from the doorway. I took a few steps inside. The bathroom was on my left. I gave it a cursory look and turned to her bedroom on my right. I saw nothing special about the furniture there, either. Then it hit me. "This could be anyone's room. It looks more like a hotel suite."

"I thought the same thing." He pointed out that there were no pictures on the walls. "It's more like a place where she lives temporarily."

"No books. No magazines," I said. "Not

even a newspaper."

"Nothing out of place, either," he said.

"She's not in her room," I said and realized how stupid the words sounded.

"So where would she be?" he asked.

When we returned to the kitchen, Simon seemed not to have moved.

We returned to the dining room, which was still empty. We assumed she hadn't gone upstairs, so that meant she must have gone outside. Just then Simon came in from the kitchen.

"Mrs. Wright isn't in her room," I said. "Do you have any idea where she is?"

He turned his face toward the back door and lifted his chin with his pointing gesture.

Tonya Borders strolled into the dining room just then. "She sometimes walks along the cliff," she said. She turned to Simon. "Is there more coffee?"

The shrug.

"Because she never leaves the island, the walk along the cliff is her only way to get away from the house," Tonya said without accent. "There is a nice little trail around the backside of the house. Have you been out there?"

After both of us said no, she said, "It's a circle of exactly three-tenths of a mile of paving stones." The Slavic accent miraculously reappeared. "When I was here in March, she told me that every morning, and again in the evening, she completes the circle three times."

Tonya went on to describe the area. Roger had a variety of azaleas — the kind that bloom in the spring and again in the fall. She rambled on about plants such as coreopsis (whatever they were), varieties of lobelia whose colors varied from white to carmine. She raved about the hybrid camellias and the highly improved impatiens. She described the poisonous Jerusalem cherry, nine varieties of ajuga, and at least a dozen types of hosta.

I tried not to yawn. I buy trays of flowers from Home Depot, and they live about three weeks before they die of thirst or starvation. I always forget about them.

"Roger wants to make sure something blooms all year long." I thought the flora lecture had reached the near torturous, but I was wrong. She had progressed to the fourteen varieties of trees on the island. Although I didn't pay much attention to what she said, it fascinated me to listen to her. I loved the accent that came and went.

"You have an interesting accent," I said. "Slavic?"

"Very good. Polish. I was born in what is

now Gdansk."

"That's near the German border, isn't it?" I asked.

"Germany borders Poland on the west, of course. Gdansk is on the Baltic Sea and at the mouth of the River Wilsa. Do you have more test questions, or must I sing to you in Polish? I came to America when I was sixteen. I have worked very, very hard to get rid of my accent, but sometimes it pops out. Is that what bothers you? I shall be glad to answer any serious questions if you doubt me."

"Yes, and I apologize," I said.

"You enjoy nature and working in the garden, do you?" Burton asked and rescued me so I could silently castigate myself.

"As a matter of fact, Roger asked me to supervise this when he had the area land-scaped."

"He used you in all kinds of ways, didn't he?" I asked.

"I resent that," she snapped. She turned and walked away.

Burton and I stared at each other. "I think we need to talk to her after we come back in," I said.

"You are direct," he said. "Very direct."

"Is that bad?"

"Different. I'm not used to that. Some

people might not like it —"

"Does Burton like it?"

He seemed to ponder the question for several seconds before he said, "I think so."

"Okay," I said. "And back to Tonya: She's suddenly quite sensitive about something."

We descended the four steps from the back door and started down the gravel path. Immediately I smelled the sage plant. I wish I could have seen the spices Roger or Tonya planted. Even though I couldn't see anything, my nose told me. I can't cook, but for some odd reason, I can identify spices. I recognized the peppery scent of savory and the fragrance of sweet marjoram. Strong breezes from the ocean seemed to fill the air with those fragrances. I paused and breathed deeply.

Aware that I had stopped, I apologized, and we started down the path. The path was a good three feet wide, so there was plenty of space for us to walk side by side.

The stars were dimmed by broken clouds, and they shrouded the moon. The smell of rain was heavy in the air, but none had yet fallen. The night clouds were at least one shade darker than when we had been out earlier.

We had gone perhaps thirty feet when I stumbled and fell into Burton. He grabbed my arm, "Hey, steady there." He took my hand and led me.

"Thank you," I said and smiled in the dark. Apparently I had done a good job on the tripping. I had decided to play it like the helpless damsel and would have worried if he hadn't responded. I liked the feel of his hand. He had stumbled at the beach, so I thought this was a good trade-off. I had perfected that tripping trick by age sixteen. In those days, I breathed deeply, sighed, stared into the boy's face, and said, "You're so strong." That line no longer seemed appropriate.

What also didn't seem appropriate was that he held my hand as he would that of anyone in distress. So far he hadn't succumbed to my charms. That was okay. I decided I'd give him another chance before we left Palm Island.

As we walked closer to the cliff, the harsh waves and the heavy wind meant we had to lean close to each other to hear. I liked that. I had to put my lips about five inches from his face. He had a faint, masculine smell, and it took me another minute to identify it. Mennen Skin Bracer. That's what my older brother used. He always said he hated the smell, but it was all he could afford. I figured Burton liked it even though he could afford better. That fragrance seemed right on him.

Despite having been on the island three times in the past, I had never been to the backside of the island and wished I could have had a daylight view. On my previous trips, I arrived from Atlanta at night. I left the next morning before daylight so I could avoid the heavy traffic going north on I-95.

I spotted a copse of oaks with Spanish moss swaying in the breeze. I counted three stunted palm trees in a sheltered area behind the oaks — just as Roger had said. We made the complete circle of the small island, but we still saw no sign of Mrs. Wright.

An involuntary shiver came over me.

7

"Let's follow the path one more time," Burton said as he started out. This time he held my elbow. I felt as if I were a tottering eighty-year-old and my grandson led me forward.

We stopped and moved into the shelter of the oaks. I didn't want to hurry back, even though I did want to talk to Mrs. Wright. In the shelter, we could hear each other without shouting. He let go of my arm.

"So, you're a reverend," I said, "and that means?"

"Pastor. Or rector or preacher — whichever feels better."

"You have a large church? I mean are there a lot of people?"

He shook his head. "I'm a shepherd, not a rancher."

"I don't get the difference. You mean you handle sheep and not horses?"

He laughed. I love it when I play ignorant

and it pays off.

"I used to be the pastor of a large church in Oklahoma. It started small — just a little more than sixty people. But it grew and grew, and after four years, we had nearly three thousand. That's when I left."

"But why? Isn't that the kind of thing most rever— I mean preachers — dream of?"

"Some might. They think that having a big church means getting more things done. I found I left more things undone."

"Didn't you have assistant priests?" (I used *priests* to show my ignorance.)

"Oh, I had four assistants, and they were fine, but that meant they got to do all the human-interest things. I conducted weddings and funerals and made a few hospital visits. You see, I'm a shepherd. For me, that means I like to know everyone by name, know where they live and what they like. When I became a rancher, I knew the names of maybe a few hundred. The rest were just people who shook my hand and called one of my assistants when they had problems."

"I suppose that gives you more time for your family."

"I don't have a family; I'm not married; I have never been married — almost got married once." He laughed. "Why is it that every time I meet an attractive woman, the first thing she wants to know is whether I'm married?"

(He said I was attractive. I liked that.) "I didn't ask if you were married."

"That would have been your next question, right?"

"You're just too quick for me," I said. I resisted batting my lashes.

"Look, you're too bright to play college-age games. I like being with you. I like you. You're bright and funny, but there's one thing we need to face right now."

"Oh, oh. You said *but,* and that's always a giveaway word."

"I like you, *but* I don't think we have a future ahead of us."

"Is something wrong with me?"

"That's not the way I'd say it."

"Oh, you can say it so it's less offensive or — ?"

"Wait — wait. I want to make sure you understand. Give me a chance, please."

"Okay, try it again." I didn't like the direction of this conversation. By now, I wanted him to be falling all over me.

"I find you attractive, and we seem to have some kind of mutual insight — some kind of connection with what's going on around here."

"So that's wrong?" I asked, now really puzzled.

"Okay, I'll say it like this. First, I'm a — well, I call myself a serious, committed Christian."

"You mean you can't listen to jokes?"

He laughed. "No, I mean I'm serious about my faith in Jesus Christ and that He's the Savior —"

"Hey, I went to Sunday school — well, maybe six times. I actually know that stuff."

"You may know about what I believe, but —"

"So, I don't believe — at least not the way you do. Is that bad?"

Burton took a slow, deep breath. I wasn't going to make it easy for him. "That's not the way I want to say it. You keep bringing in judgmental words — like bad or wrong. I'd prefer to say it this way: You and I live in different worlds." He held up his hand so I wouldn't interrupt. "Julie, forgive me if I've misled you in any way. Jesus Christ is the most important thing in the world to me. I couldn't — not ever — get serious about anyone who didn't share my beliefs."

"Oh, I see," I said. "Yeah, I guess that is bad, because I don't — I mean, I don't *not* believe exactly. It's more — more that I just never saw much use in God. You know, calling on God when you face a problem instead of handling it yourself, and then ignoring Him — or her — or it — when things go well."

"That's not the kind of Christianity I believe in," Burton said. "I don't want to tell you my life history —"

"I don't mind listening," I said.

"I don't want to tell it all, but I'll say this. I didn't grow up in the church and didn't turn to the Lord — to Jesus Christ — until I was in a pretty hopeless place in my life. I wasn't looking for a crutch as much as I needed help — ongoing help. I needed something — Someone — to guide my life. I had sure made a mess of it. I came to God out of an intense search for meaning — for purpose in living. And that's what I found."

"Is this where you tell me about how sinful you were so that I can open up and tell you what a terrible sinner I am?"

"Hey, you have been around."

I nodded. "You know why I like you, James Burton? You're different. All the other Christians — preachers, boyfriends, or my girlfriends' boyfriends — eventually got to this point and told me about burning in hell and —"

"I'd prefer to talk to you about a God who loves you — really, truly loves you," he said. "And before you interrupt again, I want to say this: I like myself. I enjoy my life. I have peace I never had before."

His sincerity sneaked through my line of defense. Okay, so I melted a little. "All right, I admit it: You're different."

"Will you think about this?" he asked. "I'd like to talk to you some more — a lot more — about the God who loves you very much."

I didn't know what to say, and without realizing it, I began to cry. "No one — no one has ever talked to me that way before."

"I didn't mean to hurt your feelings —"

I shook my head and sniffed several times. "You didn't offend me."

"I wouldn't want to hurt you. That's why I want to be clear about where I stand — where we stand."

"Let's find Mrs. Wright," I said and rubbed my tear-stained face. "I'm not ready to talk about God."

"Let's do that."

Again we circled the back side of the island, but we couldn't find her. "She might have gone back at any point, and we missed her," Burton said.

We walked back to the house. "Just one

thing, James Burton. I do like you. I don't understand your brand of Christianity — it's certainly different from the kind I'm familiar with. All anyone wanted to do was get me to the altar so I would confess all my sins."

"If you ever believe," he said so softly I had to strain to hear him, "no one should ever try to force you to do anything like that. You'll do whatever you need to do. I'm more concerned about your faith than I am about getting you inside some church building."

I took his hand, patted it, and released it. "That's why you're different. You're the first Christian who — who made me feel, well, that you care, and that maybe God truly loves me."

"I do care," he said, "and I'll tell you something else. While we were walking along, I decided that I will pray for you — every day." He turned and rested both his arms on my shoulders. "I feel we have some kind of — call it mental connection or whatever — but I will pray for you every single day. That's my promise to you. I won't bug you about Jesus Christ, but I'll always be open to talk to you about the Lord."

"I'm not sure how much I like you, James

Burton, but at least you've passed the tolerance test. Not many preacher types do."

He leaned close and kissed my forehead. "You know something? For a shrink type, you're okay, too. Just one thing —" and he laughed. "Okay, I promised I wouldn't push. I won't."

"That's the second thing I like about you." No one had ever talked to me like that before. I didn't know how to respond.

I wanted it to be clear that if I ever believed or turned to God or however they say it — I wanted it to be genuine and not just a means to get closer to Burton.

Once inside the house, we saw Wayne, Paulette, Reginald, Beth, and Tonya in the midst of some tête-à-tête in the drawing room. "Have you seen Mrs. Wright?"

All five shook their heads or mumbled negatives. They made it obvious they didn't want us to join their group. Lenny sat in a corner by himself. He looked up at us, smiled, and was ready to say something — something stupidly unfunny I'm sure — but we both hurried back out of the room and into the dining room.

We knocked again at Mrs. Wright's door, but there was no response.

"The kitchen?" Burton said, and we went there.

Simon sat on a stool and looked as if he had guarded a now-cold cup of tea for the past half hour. He shook his head before we could ask.

"But we couldn't find her out there," I said. "Come on, Simon, help us." I looked at my watch. We had gone out just before 9:20, and it was now slightly past 9:45.

"Come," he said. He left his stool, stopped at a kitchen counter, and pulled a large flashlight from the bottom shelf. "Likes walk. Stands near tree."

We followed him outside. The wind had picked up even more. Thin, sharp drops of rain struck me. I tried to say something to Burton, but he wouldn't have been able to hear me. He did take my hand, and I allowed him to lead me. So there was some compensation.

"There!" Simon shouted and pointed to a large, sprawling oak. He flashed his light on the tree. We walked up to the spot, and Burton dropped my hand. He leaned forward to examine the tree. It was fairly low, and someone had nailed four steps into the tree. I assumed Mrs. Wright climbed those steps and sat on the large, lower branch.

"Not here! Something wrong! Come!"

Simon grabbed my hand and pulled me down toward the path, and we kept going.

After maybe ten more feet, we reached the precipice. "Careful!" he said and released my hand. He stood in one spot and flashed the beam downward. I don't know much about tides, but I assumed the full tide had come and was now on its way out. Below I could see the tips of huge stones. I assumed they were there to retard the washing away of the land. I realized that we were on the high end of the island and the beach — what little existed — must have been at least fifty feet below.

For perhaps forty seconds, none of us said anything, but our eyes followed the slow, methodical sweep of the light. "See!" Simon said.

At first I saw nothing, and then I stared at the light more carefully. Burton saw where Simon pointed.

"Oh no," Burton said.

Then I saw it, too. An arm stuck out from the rocks and waves rushed over it. As the next wave receded, I saw the body.

"Come!" Simon walked rapidly another dozen feet along the cliff and pointed to a narrow, uneven path that led down. "Stay!" he said to me and started down the uneven terrain.

I didn't answer him, but I was miffed. I wasn't some heroine in a 1950s film who stood and screamed for five minutes. I jumped in front of Burton and followed right behind Simon. I didn't misstep anywhere.

As soon as he reached the rocks and had his feet firmly placed, Simon grabbed the protruding arm, reached under the cold water, found a leg, and dragged the body to the sand. Elaine Wright's body lay face down. We knelt beside her, even though the waves trickled upward and touched my feet.

The back of her head was bashed in. The sea had obviously washed away the blood, but it wasn't a pretty sight.

"Fall maybe?" Simon asked.

Burton shook his head. "I think she was hit on the head and pushed." He pointed out that she was on her stomach. Simon tried to keep the light off her head and focused on her body so we could see bruises and cuts on her arms and legs. Even though the light wasn't directly on the top of her body, I agreed with Burton. Someone had bashed in the back of her head.

"Murdered," I said softly. "A second one."

"Go. Move her higher," Simon said and made the motions of wrapping her. "Tarp. Police." He said enough that both of us understood.

"Just don't disturb any evidence," I said.

"I careful." Disdain filled his voice.

"Go on. Both of you," Burton yelled. "Simon, I'll stay beside the body until you get back."

Simon handed me the flashlight.

"I'll wait with you," I said to Burton.

"No, I want to stay here. *Alone.*"

"It's safe. After all, who would come back and —"

"I want to stay here *and pray.*"

"But she's dead. You're not going to pray for —"

"I want to pray *for the others.* For guidance. For the murderer or murderers. I need a few minutes alone."

"Sure, I guess if it helps. That's what we expect clergy types to do."

"Laypeople also pray."

By now Simon had reached the top and disappeared from view.

"I want to be alone, please," he said softly, turned away from me, and faced the ocean.

I did the Simon shrug and turned around. I made my way up the path. The sprinkling was just heavy enough to make the path slightly slippery. I shined the light at my feet and pondered what he had said. I thought about the death of Roger. Now Mrs. Wright. I agreed with Burton that someone had bashed in her head and then pushed her over the cliff. But why? What message had she tried to give someone in the room? Was it because she knew something or had seen something?

Just as I pulled myself to my feet, a lightninglike thought struck me: *Murdered.* At least one person inside the house killed two people.

A murderer? Who? Why?

I shuddered as I asked the next question aloud. "Who will be next?"

8

A killer is on the island, I thought. *No, a* murderer *is staying in the same house as I am.* I walked over to the oak, climbed the four steps, and sat down. I turned off the flashlight. I wanted to be away from everyone and think for a few minutes. The wind intensified, and more fat drops of rain struck my face, but I didn't care. I thought about each of the people inside the house and asked myself, *Who would do this? Who would hate someone enough to kill?*

Amanda said she hated her husband, and Jason didn't seem to like him, either — or said he hadn't in the past. They could have done it, or one could cover for the other. One thing for sure, all the suspects were still on the island.

Wayne Holmestead was a snake. I wouldn't put anything past him. Okay, just because I didn't like him didn't make him a killer. Dr. Jeffery Dunn might be the one, but he was so boring — or maybe he did do it. What about Paulette White or Tonya Borders? I obviously didn't like Beth Wilson, but I didn't have any feelings about her as the murderer. I sensed the carrot-headed Lenny Goss, who seemed to have a joke for everything, might be the most malevolent of them all. Reginald Ford seemed harmless enough. But then, I didn't know much about him. Maybe I simply didn't want him to be the killer.

We could eliminate Simon. He accounted for his time before he left the island to meet us, and he was with us when Roger died. Also, I'm sure he didn't leave the house while we were gone, so he couldn't have killed Mrs. Wright. I couldn't prove that, but I just couldn't believe Simon was the bad guy. I kept thinking about that wink from him. I wondered what that meant.

I pulled my thoughts back to the guests in the house. We had ten suspects. The phone wouldn't work. The storm was approaching, and it wouldn't be safe to leave the island before morning. Would there be yet another murder?

I became aware that the temperature had dropped and I felt chilled. The wind also increased. Hard spikes of cold rain struck with such sharpness that I felt as though they would nail me to the tree. I didn't care. I'd been wet before. Nearby rosebushes that had been twined around support stakes drooped, soggy and heavy with the rain.

I stayed by the tree with my thoughts until Simon returned with the tarp. I don't think he saw me; at least he didn't acknowledge me. I had the flashlight turned off. I'm not positive, but I think he was crying. He wiped his eyes just before he started down. He might have wiped away the rain, but my intuition said it was tears.

Why would Simon cry for Mrs. Wright? Or was he crying for Roger? Or both? Simon crying? That seemed odd.

I had finally had enough of the torrential downpour, so I raced toward the house. I heard footsteps behind me, looked around, and Burton was about ten feet behind me, running faster than I had.

I hurried inside and held the door open for him. "Where's Simon?" I asked.

"He'll be along."

We both stared at our wet clothes. "We need to change," Burton said.

I turned and headed toward the front of the house.

The first people we saw were Paulette White and Wayne Holmestead standing outside the drawing room. "Would you call the others into the drawing room?" Burton asked Paulette. "This is quite important."

"Are you ordering me?" Paulette asked.

"I apologize. I didn't realize I had ordered you," Burton said. "It's just that — that we have a new development, and everyone needs to know."

"Oh, that's different then." Her voice softened, and I assumed that was as close to an apology as Paulette would give anyone.

"We're both going to change clothes," I added as if that wasn't obvious. My hair felt plastered against my face, but it would dry. I have enough curl in it that I don't have to worry about doing anything with it after it's wet.

"We can use the room intercom from the kitchen," Wayne Holmestead stepped forward and said. "I'll do it."

"What is going on?" Tonya Borders asked. She had just reached the foot of the stairs. "You have no right to take over and order us around. That is the job for the police, is it not?"

"He wants us all here so you can give us a weather report and tell us that it's raining?" Paulette asked.

Burton and I rushed up the stairs. He gallantly grabbed my hand, smiled, and said,

"I don't want you to trip." He laughed.

I giggled and said, "How can I when such a strong man guides me?"

His room was across the hall from mine. We hadn't been up there, but we knew our rooms because Simon had left our luggage outside our doors. That made it simple.

I hurriedly changed and was back down in less than five minutes and went into the drawing room. Even though Wayne wanted to know what was going on, I said, "Burton will tell you."

Just then Burton came into the room. He looked around and said, "Let's wait until we're all here."

Amanda and Jason hurried into the room. Lenny hadn't gone anywhere. Paulette and Reginald stood together, speaking in whispers. With a lot of hip swinging, Beth vamped into the room. She carried a cup of tea. I suspected that Professor Dunn had waited in the dark someplace until everyone had entered. He walked inside, looked around, and slammed the door behind him.

Beth, startled, spilled her tea, but no one paid any attention. The rest of us turned and stared at Jeffery. He breathed faster than I'd ever noticed before, so that was probably meant to be a dramatic entrance.

Burton held up his hand and motioned to

indicate he wanted everyone to sit down. Simon came into the room through the doorway from the dining room. He had changed his shirt, but his shorts were soaked and he was barefooted. He must have wiped his feet, because I saw no prints on the hardwood floor.

I looked around. All twelve of us were present. Then I thought, that means if we eliminate Simon, Burton, and me, any of the remaining nine people could be the killer.

"Somebody murdered Roger Harden nearly three hours ago," Burton said, and his gaze seemed to take in everyone. "Now someone has killed Elaine Wright."

"Oh no, no," Amanda cried out. "Why? Why would anyone want to hurt her?"

"Why would anyone want to hurt Roger?" Burton asked.

"For Roger there was plenty of motive," Simon said. "All of them hated him. For Mrs. Wright, there is no motive that we know of."

"You — you spoke in full sentences!" I shrieked.

9

I stared at Simon. Was no one on the island what they seemed?

"Simon, I didn't know you knew enough English to —"

"That was part of Roger Harden's strategy. People assumed I didn't know much English, so they spoke freely. Sometimes too freely."

"Is there something you want to tell us?" Burton asked.

He shook his head. "Not yet. But if the others don't speak up and tell the truth about themselves, I may have to do some accusing."

"Would you check the phone line again?" Burton asked.

"Still dead," he said. "I checked on my way in here."

Burton nodded his thanks to Simon. "Each of you, please, tell me again about Roger and your relationship with him. Yes, this is a matter for the police, but all of you are suspects. Only Simon, Julie, and I were on our way when Roger's death occurred. We've now had a second death. We can only assume they are connected."

For several seconds, no one said anything and no one looked around. It was a strange atmosphere, almost as if no one wanted to speak, and yet everyone had something to say.

Even though we were in the windowless drawing room, we heard rain pounding against the dining room windows with increased fury. Torrents cascaded through the confines of the aluminum downspouts.

"I'll go first," Wayne Holmestead said. He attempted to look pleasant as he pulled his vest down over his stomach. "Jason and Simon haven't been kind in what they've said about me."

"Let's hear your version," Burton said.

"I agree Roger was, uh, well, controlling at times, but he was a good man. He was certainly an honest man. He was the best friend I ever had, and I loved him."

"I can say exactly the same things," Paulette White said. "Dear Roger was like a father to me. I'm only thirty-five — which is quite young to be one of four vice presidents —"

"Or perhaps not so unusual for a woman of your, uh, abilities," Amanda said.

"If you imply there was anything between Roger and me — other than business — I assure you and everyone else that is not true. I had absolutely no romantic interest in Roger. It would be like — like having an affair with my father. That is what he was like. He was my mentor and my father figure. I owed him so much. So very, very much. And I truly loved him."

"Roger planned to help me move out of weather reporting into hard news," Beth said. "He assured me that within three years, I would become an anchor in one of the major cities." She paused and looked around at us. "That certainly ought to eliminate me as a suspect."

"Unless he told you he had changed his mind," I said.

Before she could respond, Tonya Borders stood up and surveyed all of us. "I do not speak easily of emotions, but if in my heart there is any love, it was for Roger Harden."

Oh no, I groaned. This performance has to be something straight from the early talkies. Or maybe it was just a bad imitation of Greta Garbo from around 1930.

"We met — that is Roger and I — after my husband died, which was followed by the loss of my lovely daughter a few days later. Both because of an automobile accident. I did not want to live. I wanted to take my own life, but Roger came to me. He helped me want to live. He was my friend. He was my *only* friend."

The entire time she spoke, she never looked directly at any of us. For the first time I realized that she didn't make eye contact with anyone. I needed to watch that one. Something wasn't stacked right on her shelves.

"I suppose it is my turn," Dr. Jeffery Dunn said. "I teach biology classes at Clayton State University. I am tenured and have taught there for thirty years." He rambled on about his achievements and told us all about the articles he had written and the two books he had authored and that both of them had sold nearly fifty thousand copies, which was considerable for a textbook. I was half afraid he was going to pull out one of his mind-numbing articles and read it to us.

I snickered when he called himself an author. I knew the woman who had ghost-written both of them. She told me that he handed her his lecture notes and she did an immense amount of research, updated his material, and wrote both of his four-hundred-page books. He paid her well and, in fact, more than she normally would have received. The extra money was to make certain she told no one. She told me only because I was her therapist. Naturally, her work under his name became the required texts for his classes.

He rambled on and on about his achievements and finally mentioned that Roger Harden had admired his intellect and had invited him several times to visit him in his large Clayton County estates. "Five times since he moved to the island I have been privileged to have been his guest. I can only assume he respected me highly in a professional capacity, as well as regarded me as an adviser and perhaps even a close friend —"

"Uh, excuse me," Burton said. "Thank you for all the background, but tell us about your *relationship* with Roger — especially when he invited you to the island."

"I was almost to that point —"

"Get directly to the point," I said, "before we all fall asleep." That was rude of me, but he didn't seem to take offense.

"As you like." He took a deep breath. "Intimate friend may be too strong a word, but I was certainly his confidant in many matters — matters which I cannot divulge here. I don't easily employ the word *love*, and I daresay it's not quite accurate, but it is as close as any other word for the affection I felt toward him."

He started to elaborate on his emotions, but Burton thanked him and turned away from him. He faced Lenny Goss. "Why don't you tell us about your relationship."

"*Moi?* Moi?" He grinned. "I think he liked me because of my jokes."

"Doubtless," Reginald said with such venom in his voice that even Lenny couldn't have missed his meaning.

"I want you to do something, *Reggie,*" he said and grinned. "When we break up here and you go to your room, I have a small task for you. Just before you hop into your bed, I'd like you to get on your knees, close your eyes, and ponder how little your opinion means to me." He laughed and slapped his thigh. "Hey, wasn't that a good one?"

Reginald shook his head, rolled his eyes, and looked away.

"Please tell us, Lenny," Burton said. "But save the jokes, will you? We're talking about two murders."

The smile evaporated. "Yes, of course. All right, here's my story, and I'll keep it short."

"Excellent," Tonya said and smiled as if to deflect the sharpness of her tone.

"I was a literary agent when I first met Roger Harden. One of his cronies, state senator William Rice, became a client, and I represented his book. Unfortunately, I was unable to sell the book, although I sent it to fourteen publishers." He listed them by name, which impressed me that he had bothered to memorize them. "Through the Honorable Mr. Rice is how we became acquainted."

"This is the short version?" Reginald asked.

"I could go into more detail, but I'll spare you." By now it was obvious that the big jokester wasn't always a bundle of laughs.

"And your relationship with Roger?"

"Oh, it was excellent. I did all right as a literary agent, you understand, but Roger gave me one of those offers I couldn't refuse."

"What kind of offer was that? Not to turn you over to the police?" Simon said.

He glared at Simon and said, "He *invited* me to give up my agency and to work for him. He liked me, and I liked him very, very much. He felt I was — in his words — a born salesman. I'm now regional sales manager for Harden Homes in the states of Georgia, Florida, and the Carolinas. And I might add," he said and stared at Simon, "my sales have been impressive and the commissions extremely impressive."

"Even negative figures are impressive," Reginald said.

"Okay, Reginald," Burton said, "suppose you tell us about your relationship with Roger."

"Quite simple. I own a construction company. We are, uh, one of the largest in the Southeast. We build upper-scale homes — nothing less than ten thousand square feet." He smiled and said, "Much higher quality, of course, than those pedaled by Lenny."

"Okay, boys," I said. "You two don't like each other very much, but let's stay on the subject of Roger."

"Yes, yes, of course. Roger befriended me — as he did many others. He helped me out when I was, well, in a rough spot — that was years ago. I've been absolutely grateful. To show my appreciation, I have made several trips to other states on his behalf — you know, as a favor."

"A favor? Yeah, I'll bet," Jason said. "I'll bet you resented those trips."

"You seem to guess so much," Reginald said, "but you know so little."

"Jason, how about you?" Burton asked.

The boy shrugged — a gesture quite different from Simon's. He held out his hands, palms upward. "It was no secret the way I felt about Dad — my stepfather really — but that began to change almost a week ago. I don't want to talk about the details, but we had a reconciliation of sorts. I can tell you this: I used to hate him; now I love him."

"That's quite an abrupt change," Wayne said. "Perhaps too abrupt to be believable — especially when we're trying to figure out who killed my dear friend."

"Dear friend?" Jason snorted.

"Amanda, is there anything else you wish to add?"

She shook her head.

"What do you think, Simon?" I asked. Although I tried to observe everyone in the room, my gaze continued to return to him. His eyes were alert, as if he had just awakened. Brightness glowed in those soft brown eyes — as if he had just decided to join the party.

"Lies. All of you are lying." Simon stood up and shook his head. One at a time, he pointed his finger at Wayne, Paulette, Tonya, Lenny, Reginald, Beth, and Jeffery. "Why do you keep saying such things? You did not love him. You detested him. But I think I know why you insist that you loved him.

You feel you should have loved him and —"

"How dare you speak such words to me," Tonya snapped. "That is most insulting."

"I told you the truth," Paulette said.

"I am deeply and personally offended. Furthermore, I resent such a blatant, repulsive, and —"

"Be quiet, Dr. Dunn," Simon said. "I know things. I can speak up if I must."

"You — you — you —," Jeffery sputtered.

I smiled. He *could* raise his voice a full octave. I didn't know he was capable of that much inflection.

"You detested him. Every one of you hated him. At least Jason admitted it. The rest of you are first-class hypocrites."

"How dare you!" Paulette said. "You weasel, you. You think that because you acted like a dunce around here that excludes you from suspicion? How dare you say I lie?"

"Yes, I agree," Wayne said.

"You are, after all, only a servant," Reginald said, "and your whole demeanor has been a fabrication. So why should we believe you?"

"For myself, I have spoken only the truth," Tonya said as she crossed her arms in front of her and turned her gaze downward. That was the strongest accent so far.

"Hey, knock me all you want, guy," Lenny said and gave him the benefit of the defenseless grin. "I was his friend. He was mine. It's that simple."

"I certainly had no reason not to like him," Jeffery said. "He did marvelous things for my career. He helped me gain tenure a year earlier than normal and opened publication doors and —"

"Will you shut up?" Wayne said. "I can't decide if I want to fall asleep or vomit when you go into one of your long, boring speeches."

Simon shook his head but said nothing.

"Simon, you said with certainty in your voice that they hated Roger," Burton said. "You wouldn't make outlandish charges like that unless you knew something."

"That's totally correct."

"Tell us then. Tell us anything you can that you think will help."

"You ask them. I tell you they have been lying. For now I will not say anything more." He turned and started toward the door.

"Simon, please —"

The handyman stopped and turned around. "Very well. I will tell you this much. You think Elaine Wright loved Roger? Here is the truth: She hated him." He stared at

Amanda. "You thought he was kind to her?"

"I never saw him treat her badly," Amanda said. "I lived in this house, too."

"Yes, when you were around, he seemed kind, but when you were not, he was despicable. He raged over little things. He screamed one day that the clock was one minute slow as if she had slowed it down herself. Another time he went into a rampage because she served him filet of flounder when he wanted sole. He called her stupid, incompetent, and slow-witted."

"Why didn't she quit?" I asked. "She was an excellent cook and easily could have found work elsewhere."

"I can answer that in one word: *blackmail.*"

"What are you saying?" Wayne stood and walked over to him. He stopped in front of Simon and shook his finger in the man's face. "You dare to speak such things about my best friend?"

Simon took the man's finger and bent it downward. "Even now you're lying. He was not your best friend. Sit down or I may have to tell them about you."

"What? What do you mean by —"

"That's a good idea, Wayne. Please sit down, and let's allow Simon to tell us." Burton stood between the two men. He took Wayne's arm and led him to a chair.

Simon came farther into the room and stood near the fireplace so he could face everyone. "I will tell you the truth. Elaine was a criminal. If she had displeased Roger, he would have made certain that her next place to live would be a prison cell, and for a very long time."

10

"Surely you're mistaken," Amanda said. "I can't possibly believe that Elaine would be some kind of criminal."

"It's true though," Jason said. "Dad told me this earlier today — a little bit anyway."

Stunned looks filled several faces. Burton didn't appear surprised.

The room had a slight chill. Or maybe it was just something I felt. I sensed that we were moving into a new phase of the investigation — a deeper level or something. Thunder rumbled in the distance. We could no longer hear the pounding on the roof. The rain had already moved on.

"Please tell us about Mrs. Wright," Burton said. "You can't hurt her now."

"I'll tell you what I know, but I never learned the entire story," Simon said. "She told me parts of it at different times, but I know a few details."

For several minutes, Simon related a story

about an armed robbery that had taken place in Brunswick, the nearest city from Palm Island. "A man robbed a bank and walked away from the counter with a large sum of money. A woman customer tried to stop him. He shot and killed her. He raced from the bank and jumped into a waiting car. The car sped off. The driver wore a dark hood, so no one knew who it was."

"Elaine Wright was the driver?" asked Paulette.

He nodded. "They caught her brother several days later. They recovered less than half of the money, but he refused to name the driver or divulge the whereabouts of the rest. Somehow Roger found out that Mrs. Wright was the driver."

"I know how Dad found out," Jason said. "Mrs. Wright's brother is Doug Burns, and he worked in the cannery. He needed the money for an expensive procedure for his daughter. She had some rare form of cancer, and there was an experimental treatment available. He hadn't worked in the cannery long enough to have insurance, and there was also something about a preexisting condition."

Between Simon and Jason, we learned that the police tracked down Burns before he could send the money to his former wife.

"When they caught Burns, he turned over every cent he had."

"You mean they didn't recover all of the money?" I asked.

Simon shrugged. "He gave Mrs. Wright several thousand dollars. She never told me the amount. The prosecution threatened the death penalty unless he revealed the name of the driver — who would also be charged with murder and armed robbery."

"In desperation, he pleaded with his lawyer to contact Dad for him," Jason said. "Dad went to see him."

"And what did Roger do?" I asked.

"He paid for the medical procedures — some kind of transplant — it was successful, and the daughter is doing well. As for Burns," Simon said, "he received a death sentence, and Roger either couldn't do anything about it or wouldn't. He's still alive and, so far, he's lost every appeal. The governor definitely will not commute his sentence to life in prison." Simon paused and cleared his throat. He brushed his arm across his face, but not before I saw the moistness of his eyes.

He liked Elaine — I could see that. I wondered if he had been in love with her. Simon would never answer, even if I asked, but there was one question I could ask. "He said Mrs. Wright. Is there a Mr. Wright somewhere?"

"No. They divorced. She had been a highly successful chef with an impressive business in Savannah."

"That explains why she was such a fabulous cook," I said.

"She was a hard woman — really tough," Simon said. "But she had begun to thaw. Not a lot, but some. I think we were friends. At least, I tried to be her friend."

Yes, I believed that he loved her — or at least liked her a lot. The tone of his voice made it obvious to me. I glanced at Burton, and the slight raising of his eyebrow made it clear that he caught it, too. That Burton is uncanny; he should have been a therapist.

"If Burns had informed them of the identity of the driver, they probably would have commuted the sentence." Simon shook his head. "He refused and said he would never tell. Roger told Elaine he would give her a job, and he expected her to serve him well for four years. At the end of that time, he promised to return all the documentation of her guilt, help her establish a new identity, and move to another part of the country."

"But that wasn't right," I said. "She *was* a criminal."

"Yes, she was."

"Hey, that's like TV, isn't it?" Lenny said. "You know, the criminal escapes punishment for the crime and dies in another . . . Oh, I . . . Sorry."

Reginald shook his head. "You're not only despicable, but you're also an idiot."

"Now you understand why Elaine never would have quit, no matter how harsh he became. Besides," Simon said, "she had less than five months on her sentence. Her Harden sentence. That's how she spoke to me about it."

"So she wouldn't have killed him, would she?" I asked. "If she had stayed with Roger that long —"

"And he promised to turn over the evidence to her," Simon said. "I don't know what that evidence was. Elaine never told me, but she did say he had shown it to her. But I think I know."

"Then tell us," Amanda said.

"I think it was a confession written by Doug Burns, in which he detailed everything."

"Why would he do — ?"

"In return for the money for the surgery," Wayne said. "That sounds like one of Roger's methods. Humanitarian — at a price."

"So the obvious inference is that she knew something about Roger's death," Burton said. "Perhaps she saw the murderer. Is that possible?"

For what seemed like minutes, no one said a word. Simon cleared his throat and said, "I know one thing that none of you knows. And this may help move things along. I know why Mr. Harden invited each of you. I know why it was just the twelve of you."

"I've wondered about that," Burton said. "Why was it just us? Why us together? Why not others?"

"Each of you has something to hide. Each of you has a secret — a secret known only to Roger Harden."

"A secret?" Amanda asked. "What kind of secret? Do you mean blackmail or something like that? If you do, then surely — oh, you can't be serious."

"I know what I know," Simon said.

"I think that's true," Jason said. "I don't know for certain, but Dad as much as hinted at something like that. He said that for years he had enjoyed pulling the strings and making all of you his puppets."

"What did he mean by that?" asked Wayne.

"Suppose you tell us which strings he pulled in *your* life," Jason said.

"I resent that statement."

"You may resent it, Mr. Holmestead, but it's still true."

"It is *not* true. At least it is not true in my case."

"I suspect that it is true for each one of us," Jeffery said. "It is true in my life. He certainly pulled my strings. Okay, here is the truth, and I'm ready to confess. Besides, I'm sure that one way or another, it will come out: I can honestly say I'm not the least bit saddened because he is dead. I detested Roger Harden."

Even with that last sentence, Jeffery said the words with no inflection, and I almost missed the meaning. "Detested?" I heard myself ask.

"I'll say it another way then: I hated the man. I'm delighted someone finally got rid of him. Am I clearer now?"

11

"You say you hated Roger — and you say that as casually as if you were saying there will be rain tomorrow or —" Amanda choked and couldn't finish. Jason hugged her and soothed her.

"Why don't you explain?" Burton interjected. He sat next to Jeffery Dunn and stared into the passive face.

"For thirty years he blackmailed me. Can you understand my feelings — thirty years? Thirty years ago, Roger came to see me at the university. He held my dissertation in his hand."

"And that means?"

"He had learned that it was — uh, that it was not original." His hand felt around his toupee and gave it an unnecessary tug. That must have been a nervous habit.

"You mean you copied from someone?"

"Absolutely not. It was original research; however, Roger knew I had paid someone else to write it for me." He hung his head. "I was quite busily involved in private research, you see, and I didn't have time to do both, so —"

"Yeah, right!" Jason said. "The truth is you paid someone to write it for you because you weren't smart enough to —"

"That is a malicious lie! You are a detestable boy, you know." He shook his head. "But it is true that I hired someone to write it for me. I have no idea why, but she informed Roger, and he confronted me. And I have paid for my indiscretion every day of my life. Oh, not at first. No no no. He said he wanted to help me, and I agreed. But first, of course, he insisted that I sign a confession — a signed confession that he had prepared and that he promised to destroy if I 'lived a satisfactory life.' Those are the words he used — a satisfactory life — but he meant he wanted to hold the confession over me."

Tears filled his eyes. He reached up once again to straighten his toupee. "He was a deceptive man. That's what makes him so evil. At first, he was kind and I thought he was a great friend. He used his influence, and after my second year of teaching — which is unheard of at our university — he arranged for me to get tenure."

"And you liked that?" Simon said.

"I confess that I did. But I had no idea what a price I would have to pay. I became a servant to that man. If I didn't do everything he asked — everything, even trivial things — he said he would expose me."

"What did he ask you to do?" Burton asked.

"Mostly meaningless things. I frequently came in answer to a summons to his home in Clayton County and later, after he moved permanently, to this island. Five times he asked me to break into the university's computer system — which I did. He never asked me to change anything. He simply wanted to know confidential data. I supplied him with information about the university staff and, well, about anyone else I heard about. Eight times he had me break into the president's personal e-mail. I became his personal messenger to pass on gossip or any kind of private, sensitive communication. He was detestable."

"Which would give you a strong motive to kill him," I said.

He shook his head. "Absolutely not. I came here to confront him — but not to kill him."

"We have only your word for that," Wayne said. "I think you need to give us more convincing information — some proof of what you say."

We waited while Jeffery cleared his throat and shifted his skeletal weight several times. "I am fifty-nine-years-old, and at the end of this school term, six weeks ago, I became eligible for retirement."

"So you thought you could make Roger back off?" I asked.

"No, not that. You see, I went to the president just before the end of the term. I confessed to him what I had done — about the dissertation, I mean. He doesn't know about anything else. I certainly never told him about Roger's extortion."

"And the result?" Burton asked.

"The president said I could retire and there would be no repercussions. I had to endure a stern lecture by him. I think he was glad to get rid of me. He has never liked me very much, and it was an easy way to push me out of the system without any problems for him. I accepted Roger's invitation so I could spit in his evil face."

"Did Roger know why you agreed to come?"

"No, although I whispered to him during teatime that I wanted — that I *needed* — to talk to him privately."

"I heard him say that," Amanda said.

"Roger said he would see him after dinner."

"It was a little more than that," Jeffery said. "In fact, it was rather — how shall I say? Cryptic. He said that he had a significant announcement to make at the end of dinner. If I still wanted to talk to him, I could do so after that. I wondered if he meant he would expose me —"

"So that would have given you a motive," Paulette said.

"*Au contraire.* It absolves me. I had nothing more to fear from him. I was ready to confront him, yes, and tell him how despicable he was. In fact, I looked forward to telling that old devil that I was no longer his slave."

His words were powerful, but typical of the man, they were spoken in such a monotone he might have discussed a feature he had seen on TV.

"I did not kill him," he said, and then he raised his voice and emphasized each word: *"I did not kill him."*

"Thank you," Burton said. "Dr. Dunn, I appreciate your honesty." He patted Jeffery on the shoulder as he might gently touch a child. Burton looked around at the rest of us. "Is there anyone else who wants to speak?"

"I'll tell you," Beth said. "It's all written

down someplace. And if someone has that information, I suppose it will come out." She told about her life before she got on television. She had never been married, and she had used recreational drugs regularly. Because of her drug use — and she insisted she had never been addicted or been in rehab — she had served a year in prison for "selling myself," as she put it.

She changed her name to Beth Wilson with forged documents. "Roger found out, and I have no idea how he learned the truth. That was nearly a year ago. Since then, he has controlled my life."

As I listened, I felt sorry for her. Maybe I had been jealous of her gorgeous hair and smooth skin. As I listened, I realized that she hid a lot of pain behind that constant smile.

Burton thanked her for being honest with all of us.

"You might as well speak up," I said. "You all have something you're holding back."

"Okay, you might as well hear my story now," Lenny said. "I'm not proud of what I've done, but it's over, and I didn't kill Roger."

"Make us believe that," Reginald said.

12

"Tell us your story," Burton prompted Lenny.

He looked around at us, dipped his chin, and said, "I told you earlier that I was a literary agent, and that's true. Or perhaps it's better to say that's what I called myself in those days. I had an office in Savannah and a post office box and even a toll-free number."

He put his hands together, palm against palm, held them up to his chin, almost as if he were a child at prayer. His green eyes looked so sad. For the first time, I felt sorry for him, and I didn't even know what he had done.

"I called myself a literary agent. I worked mostly through the Internet. I paid for those huge pop-up ads that told people I could help them publish their book. Very slick, very professional looking. Why wouldn't they be? I paid plenty for them to look first class. I used the ploy that everyone has at least one book inside them. You probably saw the ads."

Because none of us seemed to know about them, I think that disappointed Lenny.

"Uh, well, I actually ran a scam," he said. "Yes, it's true: I did. I cheated people."

I stared at him. Did he think we wouldn't believe him capable of such a thing?

"It worked like this. They read my ads that said I would get their manuscripts to a publisher and help them get published. They paid me five hundred dollars to read the material, because I assured them that's how I'd know how and where to sell it."

"I know how the rest of that goes," Reginald said.

"Maybe you do." Lenny explained that even without reading a story — he never looked at any — he told every want-to-be writer that his or her manuscript still needed work. "I told them they had great ideas but the book wasn't publishable as it was. I made a big point of saying that the material had great potential but it still needed professional fine-tuning." He stopped and smiled at all of us as if he expected us to applaud his brilliant scheme.

No one responded.

Lenny sent each one a personalized letter

(meaning he inserted a personal note here and there on his form letter) and said he worked closely with an editing service. He was in Savannah and the editing service was supposedly in New York. That was the come-on, because the material was sent to a Manhattan post office box and then forwarded to Lenny's sister, who also lived in Savannah.

"My sister did edit — a little — before she returned the manuscripts in large packages to her friend who picked them up at the same Manhattan post office. Each of them was addressed, stamped, and mailed from New York. We wanted to make sure the clients could see a Manhattan postmark on the envelope. Clever, right?"

Again, no one responded, and once again he looked deflated.

Lenny wrote the client and said he had received an edited copy from the editing service and made the clients an offer. For a thousand dollars, he would send their manuscripts to twenty publishers; for twenty-five hundred dollars, he would send it to fifty.

He laughed. "Most of them wanted fifty publishers to see it."

"And no editor ever saw the manuscripts," Burton said.

"Correct. This is the beauty of the scheme. We sent them rejection slips — maybe five or ten at a time, and from our office. They looked exactly like stationery from bona fide publishers." He grinned and slapped his knee. "It was a great system. You see, I had sent manuscripts to each of the publishers, received rejections, and made new stationery from their letterheads." He paused, I suppose, for us to absorb his brilliant scheme. "I thought that was an excellent touch. Most scams wouldn't go that far. Perhaps that's why I was so successful."

"How did Roger find out?" I asked.

"Earlier this evening, I mentioned that one of my clients had been William Rice, a state senator. One day he boasted to Roger that he expected a contract for his memoirs from a New York publisher."

"And Roger didn't believe it?"

"Believe it!" Lenny slapped his knee again. "That idiot Rice couldn't write five grammatical sentences. My sister thought it was one of the worst manuscripts we'd ever received."

Lenny said that Roger tracked him down and informed him that he had violated federal law because he used the postal service. Of course, Lenny knew he had violated federal laws. "I thought I had everything covered so that no one could detect any wrong — okay, any fraud."

Roger threatened to expose him and then offered his silence for a price.

"So what was your slave contract with him?" Jeffery asked.

Lenny said that Roger hired a ghostwriter to revise the manuscript and induced a regional publishing house to accept William Rice's book. "Rice got his book, loved it, and never learned how it came about. It sold well. He pushed all his friends to buy a copy — I think he sold something like twelve thousand copies. And for a lousy book like that, anything more than fifty copies would have been remarkable."

"But what price did you pay? What did Roger demand of you?" I asked. "There always seemed to be a price for his generosity."

"Total control. That's all. I gave up the literary business and went to work for him. I also, uh, spied on other employees, and I let him know anything I heard about his competitors in other areas. I did a little industrial espionage for him. You know, I'd find out what products a corporation planned to produce and someone — I don't know who — either stole or copied the information and allowed one of Roger's companies to beat the competition. That kind of thing."

"And you hated doing that?" I asked.

"Not at first. For a year or so, it was fun — really — but I realized that Roger was never going to let me go. The more I did for him, the more evidence he stacked against me."

"Sounds like a good motive for murder," Jeffery said.

"Maybe, except that I didn't kill him. I hated him, but I liked the work — the real work — the sales. I make good money, even if he forced me to do a few, let's say, unsavory things."

"What about the rest of you?" I asked.

"Go ahead and tell him, Reggie, old boy," Lenny said. "I can and I will if you don't. You see, I know your story — or at least enough to embarrass you if you don't speak up."

In that moment, it became obvious why the two men disliked each other. Not only did Lenny know, but he had made sure Reginald was aware of what information he had.

"I suppose I should. If I don't, this loud mouth will tell you and intentionally distort everything."

"Then let's hear your version," Burton said.

Reginald reminded us that he owned a prestigious construction firm. He had figured out a way to skim a few dollars off so that the government wouldn't know. He also bilked a few wealthy clients. He banked the extra profits in the Cayman Islands.

"How few dollars?" I asked.

Reginald ran his hand through his prematurely white hair. "Uh, quite a lot as a matter of fact."

"About sixteen million dollars?" Lenny said.

"That's quite untrue. It was less than half that amount."

"Sixteen," Lenny insisted.

"All right, let's *say* sixteen million, but —"

"How did Roger find out?" Simon asked.

"I told him."

That statement surprised all of us.

"I told him because I was desperate. You see, I had three accounts set up, but they were actually bogus." He went into a lengthy explanation that was almost as dull and circuitous as listening to Dr. Dunn. It was getting late, I had had a long day, and (to be truthful) my mind wandered. But I did get the final pitch.

Auditors uncovered the fact that two million dollars was missing from one client. Reginald said he had the money in a safe-deposit box. He gave some kind of explanation to the auditors about his reasoning that was supposed to make sense, but they were skeptical — naturally. It was something to the effect that the client was paranoid and might demand the money in cash at any time, and Reginald felt he needed to keep the account liquid. As crazy as that sounded, the auditors said they would come the next day to collect the fund and deposit it properly. He asked them to come after three o'clock and he'd have the money.

"I called Roger and pleaded with him. I said I had to have two million dollars in cash before three o'clock tomorrow." Reginald smiled momentarily. "He said that although it would be a little inconvenient to get that amount of money in cash, he could do it and would have it delivered to my office by noon. He was true to his word. Messengers brought the money in five briefcases, mostly in hundred-dollar bills. They went with me to my bank where I deposited the money."

Reginald went on to tell us that the auditors threatened to report him for such a business practice. That would mean a jail sentence and a huge fine. "I called Roger again, and he came through a second time. I don't know what he said to them or what transpired. I know only that one of the auditors phoned me the next day and said they were satisfied and would not make any complaint."

After that Roger called Reginald regularly — sometimes as often as once a week — and asked him to make trips for him. "Can you believe that one time he made me travel all the way to Seattle to bring back a shipment of fresh salmon? He could have had them shipped faster than it took me to go there, collect them, and bring them back."

"Control," Wayne said. "That was his forte all right. Just control."

"And you speak from experience?" I asked.

He shook his head. "I knew of several people. That's all."

"Are you sure it's only other people you know about?"

"I told you, I was Roger's friend — maybe his best friend."

"Or his best puppet," said Jason.

"Do you have anything to tell us?" Burton asked.

"I do not."

Neither did anyone else.

"Suppose we adjourn for the night?" Burton asked. "Is there anyone who's afraid?"

"All the bedroom doors can be locked from the inside," Amanda said. "Jason has a connecting room next to mine. He and I will get up and have breakfast by 7:30. By then, we hope the phone will work."

Within two minutes, everyone had left except Burton and me.

"I'm not sure what is going on," I told him, "but I'm grateful to Roger Harden. He has been tremendously helpful to me personally and to my career."

"Really?"

"Absolutely. That's why I wanted to come. I wanted to thank him." I told Burton about three specific programs Roger had started before I went into private practice, and how he helped me establish two humanitarian programs afterward. One of them was to give special tutoring to children of poor families that needed help. The other was his privately funded program where women could learn retailing or simple office work and be paid while they learned.

Burton listened without a word. I liked that. As I talked, I kept thinking, he actively listens just by the use of his eyes. Something about the intensity of his gaze made me know he heard every word.

He also had that rare ability to invite intimacy — I don't mean sexual intimacy — something deeper, more personal. He didn't blink or look away. It was almost as if his dark eyes bored into mine and invited me to open myself to him. I wish I had that ability. If I had, I suppose it would become a technique or a gimmick. The interesting thing about James Burton was that he didn't seem to know what a gift he had.

"Very interesting," he said. "But what about the other kind of help he gave you?"

I stared at him in confusion. "What do you mean?"

"The blackmail. The threat of exposure. He held it over the others. What about you?"

"What about you? You tell me first. Why did you come to the island?"

"I have no idea what he wanted," Burton said. "Roger phoned me a week before I received the invitation. He said he wanted to thank me for being a friend to Jason. The three of us had planned to go snorkeling tomorrow."

I focused on his eyes; I didn't think he was lying.

"So what about you?" he asked. "You don't have to tell me, but there is something — something he held over you, isn't there?"

I felt my eyes widen. "How do you know that?"

"I'm not sure," he said and gave me that full-teeth grin that melted me.

"You're not going to say that God told you about all my past sins, are you?" I laughed. "That would at least be a good line. No one ever used that one on me."

"Call it intuition. Call it experience, I honestly don't know. I'm a pastor and I do a little counseling. You know, people come to see me all the time. I listen, and over the years I've developed what I call my truth antennae. I often seem to know when people lie — not all the time — but usually when they try hard to make me believe something that's a definite fabrication."

"Okay, so what about Dr. Dunn? What he told us, do you think that was true?"

"Most of it. I believe Roger blackmailed him. I suspect there is more to it than what he told us — something a little less tasteful."

"I agree with you there. Do you want to know what I think? I think he stole his dissertation. He stole it from somebody, made a few cosmetic changes, and passed it off as his own."

"I agree. I can't tell you how I knew, but I was sure he didn't buy it."

"You're very good, Burton."

"So are you, especially when you want to evade an answer."

"Was I that obvious?"

"You're very good at evasion. I'll bet that's how you hold people off when they try to pry. You throw a question at them."

"Is that what you think?"

Burton laughed. It was a good full laugh, and I enjoyed watching him. There was nothing pretentious about it. He was quick, and he didn't miss anything.

"It's a long story," I said.

"It's a long night." He leaned back into the sofa and patted it for me to sit at the other end. "I assure you that I won't fall asleep while you talk."

"I'm innocent of murder, and you're my alibi. That's obvious, isn't it?"

"Simon is your alibi, too," he said. "But you're saying then, that you're guilty of something but not of murder. Is that correct?"

"Yes."

"Of what are you guilty?"

"It doesn't matter. Not now," I said. "Why do you want to know?"

"Ah, evasion again. Good! Wait a minute. Are you saying that you had a motive for killing him?"

"Absolutely."

13

"I said it was a long story." That was another evasion, but I should have known Burton wouldn't be put off.

"I like long stories." Burton leaned just slightly forward. "Please trust me, Julie. Anything you say, I promise to hold in absolute confidence."

"Isn't that what we say to clients when they're skittish?"

He didn't respond to my evasion. I stared at him for several seconds, although it seemed like minutes. I wanted to tell him because I had never told anyone before, and it was a burden I had carried too long. Most of all, I was too ashamed to tell the truth.

As if reading my mind, he said softly, "Sometimes we let fear or shame hold us back. And as long as we hold it inside, we're never free." He got up from the sofa and said, "I'm going to get iced tea or whatever there is to drink in the kitchen. May I bring you something?"

I nodded because I didn't trust my voice. I wanted to tell him. *But what if he doesn't like me afterward?* I thought. *What if he thinks I'm a terrible person?* As I heard those words inside my head, I thought of my own counseling situations. If clients said those words — and they sometimes did — I would have answered much like Burton, and I would have urged them to expel their demon by talking.

I picked up two pillows, pulled them in front of me, and huddled against the sofa. *Can I tell him? Can I trust him? Will he understand?* I wanted to explain everything to Burton, but I wasn't sure I had the courage.

He brought in two glasses of iced tea, pulled up a small table, and set mine down. He sipped his tea but said nothing.

I still wrestled with my inner voice. I opened my mouth, and once the words started, it became remarkably easy to talk to him.

"I was married once," I said. "I married when I was barely eighteen, and my husband was twelve years older than I was. I loved him — or perhaps I should say I loved the man I thought he was. He seemed sweet, charming, and thoughtful. I never detected who he really was until we had been married two months."

I paused and stared at Burton.

"As I've already said, I like long stories," he said.

Julie had met Dana Macie during her first year of college. It had been one of those whirlwind romances and marriages. Dana came from a moneyed family. He told her he was a freelance businessman, but he never explained exactly what he did. She knew only that he always had money and didn't seem to have regular business hours. He was sometimes gone for two or three days at a time, and when she asked, all he said was, "It's just business."

She was young, impressionable, and very romantic. He was six five, blond, with a broad chest and narrow waist and hips — almost like a man with a sculptured body. Her girlfriends all but swooned whenever Dana came around. When she looked back, she realized that the reaction of other women had been a strong motivation for accepting his attention and saying yes when he asked her for dates. Other women envied her, and she liked that.

Julie had grown up in Villa Hills, Kentucky, a small town near Cincinnati, and gone to college in Georgia to get away from an unhappy home situation — a dominating stepmother and a docile father.

She and Dana met in late November, dated most of December, and married in January. No one in her family attended the wedding. Her stepmother wrote, "This is a most inconvenient time for a wedding, so we shall not attend." Just that note and nothing else. Not a phone call or e-mail. They didn't send a gift.

Dana tried to comfort Julie and promised he would be all the family she ever needed. She believed him because she wanted to believe he could wrap his arms around her and take away her rejection and hurt.

One thing about Dana bothered Julie: He drank — not much, but regularly. It was as if he had to have at least one (and usually it was two or three) drinks every night.

After they married, his drinking increased. He drank an expensive brand of scotch and grumbled if she didn't restock before he needed more. At first, she ignored the liquor. Then she tried to be subtle and asked him to cut down. He laughed and said, "I'll think about it." After that, his drinking increased.

The crisis came at an afternoon cocktail party in early April. His friends had decided to throw a belated party to celebrate their wedding. To please her husband, Julie drank half a glass of chardonnay, but she didn't enjoy it. He insisted on a second, so she let him pour her one. After she took a sip, he kissed her on the forehead and walked away. An hour later, Dana realized the glass was still full. "You haven't touched your wine." He stood in front of her and said, "Cheers and bottoms up."

She took a tiny sip.

He smiled and leaned toward her. "Bottoms up."

"I've had my limit."

"Drink it. *Now.*" The smile was gone and a hard look filled his face. Dana had never spoken to her in such a tone before.

She gulped down the second drink, even though she had to force it. She set the empty wine glass on the table. "It's — I guess I just don't like this. You know, I'm not used to drinking."

Dana left and returned almost immediately with a bottle. "This is mavrodaphne, a sweet Greek wine and difficult to find in most parts of the country." He opened the chilled bottled and filled her glass. "I have a special source, and I share this vino with few people."

"I really don't —"

"Just drink it." He touched her hand, and his voice became gentle again. "You'll like it."

She brought the glass to her lips and held it there as she tried to think of an excuse not to drink it.

"Just drink it."

"But, darling —"

Dana said nothing. He stood in front of her until she drained the glass.

"It's sweet, but I don't really like —"

"You can learn to like it." His voice had a slight edge to it. As soon as she finished it, he poured her another.

"No, that's really enough," she said. She forced a laugh. "You don't want to carry me out of here."

"It's not enough. You're still too uptight."

Julie had never been drunk. She had learned a number of tricks over the few months of their marriage to avoid taking more than a few sips. One was to pour the wine into a nearby receptacle or stroll outside and pour it over the balcony. A few times she dumped the drink into the toilet, flushed it down, and sprayed the room with air freshener.

This time Dana stayed only a few feet away and watched her. He insisted she finish each glass. It was as if he made it a personal crusade to get her drunk. While he watched, he drank at least ten glasses of scotch.

"I don't want any more," she said after the fourth drink. "Please, Dana. My head is spinning."

"It's not spinning enough," he said. "I know your tricks to avoid having a good time. I like to drink, and I want to share all the good things in my life. I enjoy living this good life and —"

"You call this enjoying life?"

"It used to be fun."

"Used to be?"

"Yeah, it was until I married you."

"I didn't force you to marry me," she said. She set her drink on a table and staggered from the room. She had to get outside and into the air. The room, filled with people, loud music, billows of cigarette smoke, loud talking and laughing, made her feel trapped.

She walked over to the patio door, and she had to hold on to the building to retain her balance. The early evening sky had changed from gold to apricot and orange. As she watched, shards of gray streaked through the flaming colors as if to say, "The night has almost come." She watched the clear lines of the hills fade away. The land-scape seemed ready to sleep. She inhaled the fragrance from the nearby magnolia tree. If she could stay outside long enough, perhaps the dizziness would go away.

She had no idea how long she stayed on the patio. She closed her eyes and tried to shut out everything. After what seemed like a few minutes, although it may have been longer, she heard someone come up behind her; she didn't turn around.

"Don't be that way, darling." Dana stood behind her and ran his fingers across the back of her hand. "I'm sorry. Sometimes I do dumb things."

Julie didn't move or say anything.

He wrapped his arms around her. She wanted to lean back and let him hold her as he'd done so many times, but something was different. Perhaps it was the way he held her. Then she realized what it was: He also tapped one foot.

Afterward when she thought about it, the moment seemed ludicrous. While he begged her to forgive him, he tapped his foot impatiently as if to ask, "How long is this going to take?"

Without turning around, she asked "What's wrong?"

"Nothing you can't change," he said gruffly. "Just loosen up. This is party time. We're supposed to be the guests of honor.

This is a party my friends set up for us —
to celebrate our wedding. Get it? To celebrate? That's what we're trying to do, and
you desert everyone."

"I doubt that anyone has noticed —"

"*I* noticed. That's what counts, isn't it?"

"How can you change so quickly from
warm to cold?"

Dana laughed. "Maybe that's part of my
charm." He kissed the back of her neck.
"Now I want you to take my arm and smile,
and let's go back inside and I'll give you a
fresh drink."

"I've had enough," she said.

He whirled her around so that she faced
him. He gripped her left arm. "Listen to me
and listen with your full attention. I've put
up with you for a long time. I'll tell you
when to stop drinking. You want to spoil
every party and every fun time. No more,
babe. No more. Got that?"

"You're hurting me," she said.

He tightened his grip, grabbed her other
arm, and squashed her against his massive
chest. "I'll hurt you more unless you do
what I say." He pulled tighter.

She tried to push away, but he pinned her
arms to her side. She could hardly breathe.

"Will you do what I ask?" He pulled her
tighter still.

She nodded as she gasped for breath.

Slowly he released her, and she took several deep gulps of air. She tried to look into his face, but it was too dark on the patio to see his features. "What is going on? This isn't the Dana I married, or is this the real Dana?"

"Just shut up. Get back inside. I expect you to enjoy yourself as much as I do. Got that?"

He turned and walked back into the party. A full minute later, one of their hosts came out with a glass of red wine for her. "Dana told me to bring you a drink. Here it is. Nice and chilled." She handed it to Julie and added, "If you want anything stronger, let me know."

Julie grabbed the glass and drank the contents in one long swallow and handed back the glass.

She brushed past the woman, went inside, and drank another.

Julie could think only of oblivion. She didn't want to see the people or hear their mindless chatter or cough whenever someone blew cigarette smoke her way. A distinct odor drifted her way. At first she thought it was some kind of spice, but it wasn't one she recognized. It had a strong, sweetish aroma. She'd never used marijuana, but she spotted four people in the far corner. They smoked, and she heard words such as *toke, hit,* and *joint.* Classmates in college had used those words, so now she knew.

What are we doing at a party like this? Who is this man I married? What is going on? He's never been this way before. Is it because he's drunk?

A moment of reality slipped through the haziness. She dropped into a nearby sofa and closed her eyes. *No, this is the real Dana Macie. The man I dated was an actor, an imposter.* She closed her eyes. *How blind could I have been?*

"Wake up!"

Rough hands shook her, and Julie opened her eyes. Immediately she felt dizzy. Dana pulled her to her feet, and she held on to him so she could stand. "The party's over and it's time to leave."

"Leave?" she asked numbly. "Where am — ? Oh, the party."

Dana pulled away from her and headed toward the front door. She tripped over an empty bottle and upturned an ashtray. She stumbled into a crystal serving tray, and glasses fell to the floor and shattered. A few feet away, a man lay on the floor, a stupid grin on his face, and he sang to himself.

Julie's body felt fully relaxed, and she only

wanted to sleep. But she had to move — and to keep on moving. She had to tell herself, move your right foot. Move your left. After what seemed like minutes, she reached the door. Dana had left it open, and a cool breeze struck her face.

"Ah!" She inhaled the blowing air. Not only did she detect the magnolia, but a scent of honeysuckle filled her nostrils. Ordinarily the cloying odors were too much for her, but tonight it rallied her senses. She stood straight and willed away the dizziness. She walked slowly down the five steps to the driveway. Dana had pulled their Mercedes convertible fairly close. Although she felt lightheaded, she was able to walk.

The day had been warm but overcast, and now fog crept along the street. She felt as if it had thickened while she watched. She peered at the street lights that seemed to compete with the gathering murkiness. They were in Henry County, about forty-five miles from their house, in a low-lying area where they often received heavy fog before and after rain. She felt a few drops of moisture on her hand.

"Will you hurry up?" Dana abruptly got out and came around to where she stood. He thrust the key into her hands. "You drive. I'm too mellowed out."

"I'm not fit to —"

He grabbed her by the throat. His fingers dug deeply into her skin. "Maybe you didn't hear me. You drive!"

"Okay," she said. She threw her purse into the backseat of their convertible and drove off. They had at least an hour's drive to reach the southeast side of Atlanta.

Dana fell asleep almost as soon as he got back into the car. He snored gently from his side. After they passed the vast houses in the wealthy community where they had partied, she drove along a long stretch of highway that would eventually lead to I-75. The fog grew denser as she drove. With her lights on, she could see only a short distance ahead of her and rarely more than twenty feet. She had started out at fifty-five but slowed to forty miles an hour. She eased up on the gas pedal until the speedometer registered thirty. Her hands gripped the wheel, and she felt the strain from leaning forward.

Her stomach roiled, and bile snaked its way to her throat. Several times she wondered if she would have to stop and vomit. Her palms sweat, and she wiped them on her skirt. Sweat trickled out of her armpits and down her sides. The rope of nausea in her stomach knotted tighter.

Julie slowed to twenty. At that speed her headlights barely illuminated the yellow lines ahead. For the next nine miles, the road curved badly. The yellow diamond-shaped sign showed the snake icon and said thirty miles an hour. That was the speed limit for good weather.

She feared that she would run into a ditch. Another mile, and she realized that rain had come and gone in that area. The roads were shrouded with a thick mist, and the highway was silvery wet. Even going twenty-five, she misjudged and the right tire went off the pavement. She jerked the car back onto the road.

Dana awakened, rubbed his eyes, and blinked at the speedometer until he could read the numbers. "I told you to drive, not *coast* down the road." He scooted toward her until his foot reached the gas pedal. He kicked her foot aside and pressed on the accelerator. The car spun forward. She tried to stay in the middle of the road, but the fog was too heavy for her to judge properly. She crossed the double yellow lines on every curve.

"Please take your foot off —" she yelled and realized that was a mistake.

Dana pressed harder. "Don't tell me what to do. I tell you. Now drive and shut your mouth." He closed his eyes and swore at her.

Julie leaned forward and tried to peer through the massive clouds of fog. She had no idea how long she drove. Three times the right front wheel went off the road. So far they hadn't encountered any cars coming toward them.

She had no idea where they were, and Dana's foot didn't let up on the pedal. They were down to less than a quarter tank of gas, and she hoped they'd run out of gas. But a quarter tank would probably take them all the way home.

She may have fallen asleep; she may have only blinked. Julie would never know which. A sudden crash, and the next thing she knew, she lay on the ground outside the car. It took her a few seconds before she was aware enough to get up. Nothing seemed broken, but whenever she moved, her body ached in a new spot. She crawled to the front of the car and slowly pulled herself upright.

To her surprise, the car lights still worked. The vehicle had climbed nearly three feet up a magnolia tree and hung there. Because of the impact, the tree leaned backward. She hobbled to the driver's door. Dana's body had fallen over on her side, the door was open, and he hung face down. His face was covered with blood.

She felt for a pulse.

There was none.

14

Julie didn't know what do. It must have been close to three o'clock in the morning by then. The fog slowly drifted away, and she could finally see the road. Ahead she spotted a sign that pointed Macon to the left and Stockbridge to the right. At least she knew where she was.

She found her purse on the floor in the backseat and pulled out her cell phone. They were less than three miles from Roger Harden's massive estate — it was huge, several hundred acres. Roger and her dad had been good friends when they were young and were classmates through high school. As a favor to her Dad, she had called Roger when she first enrolled at Clayton University. Roger visited her several times, took her to dinner, and insisted she keep his number. "If you ever need anything — anything — just call me," he said.

Julie fumbled through the address book in

her purse until she located his number. She didn't know what else to do except call Roger. Her hands shook so badly she had trouble dialing and had to start over.

Dana's dead, her mind said. *You killed him. He's dead.*

"Noooo," she cried and finally punched in the right number for Roger Harden.

"I killed him! I killed my husband — I was driving and he put his foot on the pedal and I couldn't see and —"

"Calm down," Roger said in a soothing voice. "Please relax. Tell me where you are." He talked for at least two minutes, and she did calm down.

"I'll be there. Don't do anything; don't touch anything."

Roger arrived at the crash within ten minutes. Julie walked around slightly dazed, afraid that if she stopped moving, she'd lie down and go to sleep. Roger walked up — held up his hand, and said, "Let me look it over." He stood at the side of the car and carefully took in everything. Finally, he said, "Dana was driving."

"No, I was — I told you —"

He came up close and stared into her eyes. "Listen to me, Julie. Dana was driving. He was drunk, but he insisted on driving. Is that correct?" She tried to explain what

Dana had done about the gas pedal, but he motioned for her to stop talking.

"You have not been listening," Roger said.

He pulled Dana's body over so it was fully in the driver's seat. He opened the passenger door, applied pressure, and bent it so it wouldn't close. He grabbed her purse and threw it on the ground on the passenger side. "Stand over here when the police arrive," he said. Then he dialed 911.

"So that's the horrible story," I said. "Roger covered it up for me. I was charged with nothing. I might have been acquitted anyway, but I don't think so. I was driving under the influence, and Dana died. That is a crime.

"Roger has held that accident over my head for the past seven years. He never wanted money — Roger wasn't that kind of extortionist. He wanted power — he had to have control in my life. I didn't realize until I got here that I wasn't his only victim."

"I'm sorry," Burton said.

"In case you wonder, I've never had a drink since. And I have no desire for one — I didn't before, but I drank just to please him. After Dana's death, I learned a number of things about him."

"Such as?"

"I learned he was into drugs — really into them. I found them hidden all through the house. He had more than fifty bottles of Ecstasy. I found several pounds — I guess you call them kilos — of marijuana. He had nineteen bottles of prescription drugs — all of them some kind of speed." She laughed self-consciously. "I was so naïve, I had to look the drugs up on the Internet to know what they were."

"What did you do with them?"

"I flushed them down the toilet. It took me exactly nine flushes to get rid of everything."

"You had no idea about his other life?"

I shook my head. "None. I also began to receive phone calls — on his cell. People wanted a fix, or usually they'd say they wanted a little help. I told them to hang up or I'd call the police. After a few weeks, they stopped calling."

"I went back to my maiden name of West to get away from that whole scene and especially from Dana's friends or customers or whatever they were."

"And Roger took care of everything with the police?" Burton asked.

"Everything. He took over, and I have to say I was glad. He told the police he had been driving by, heard the crash, and rushed

170

to our aid. He said he knew Dana, which he didn't, and he also told them he had heard that my husband drank a lot, and he said that he had even observed him drunk once in public. In Georgia, the legal limit is .08. Dana's was almost twice that amount. Worse, they found he had several prescription painkillers in his bloodstream as well as marijuana.

"After Roger spoke to the police, no one ever questioned me. Roger brought me to his house. I stayed in shock for most of the next week. That's when I met Amanda and Jason, and they were extremely kind to me. Eventually the police chief came to Roger's house to see me. 'Sorry, ma'am, that you had to be involved, but the world is better off without him.' That was it. I never had anyone ask me anything else."

I filled in a few more details, but Burton had already figured it out. "Roger had taken pictures before he moved Dana's body. He threatened to show the pictures to the police if I ever gave him any problems. 'Murder has no statute of limitations,' he reminded me.

" 'But it wasn't murder,' " I insisted.

" 'It will be if you cross me,' he said. He also told me that he could 'enlist half a dozen people' to testify to our fights and arguments and that I'd threatened to kill Dana on more than one occasion.

" 'But there were no fights,' " I protested. " 'I never threatened him — not ever.'

" 'Perhaps,' Roger said, 'but I can assure you that no one will believe you.' That's when I realized he would do anything to keep me under his control."

"And what did he ask you to do?"

I couldn't look at him, because I was embarrassed to admit it. "I was a spy — like Dr. Dunn. He had someone show me how to break into the county mental health files. He also showed me how to gain undetectable access to the files of eight psychiatrists."

"And you reported — ?"

"Only information that he demanded. I never volunteered. Roger didn't know it, but I held back as much information as I could," I said. "But yes, I did a totally unethical thing. I was one of Roger's robots."

After I finished my confession, Burton and I stared at each other. I felt the sympathy pour from him, but he didn't say anything. Finally, he took my hand, patted it, and said, "Please forgive me. I had no idea —"

"It's all right. I've held it in all these years,

and I truly needed to tell someone. Thank you for being that someone."

Burton hugged me then. No kiss. No magic moment. Just a hug. But it was warm and tender, the kind given when we want to comfort someone who hurts. I've been out with enough men to know the difference. I felt as if he cared about *me.* I could have been a woman of seventy or a boy of fourteen and the hug would have been the same.

As he held me, I realized that the demons of shame and embarrassment were — if not gone — at least greatly diminished.

We sat next to each other on the sofa like that until my tears began. I had no idea they were coming, but it was like an unexpected eruption. I cried with a lack of self-consciousness and control that I hadn't experienced since I had been a child.

Burton released me, and I stared at his moist eyes. He had felt my pain. That brought even more comfort. No one had ever felt my pain before.

Then the convulsive sobs began. I have no idea where they came from, but I couldn't stop them. More tears came — tears I had not shed at Mom's funeral, at Dana's, or at any other time in my life. It felt as if everything came together at once. My body shook, and I wept until I thought I would never stop shaking with the sobs and the grief — and especially from the guilt. Wisely, Burton didn't touch me; he didn't need to. He provided a safe environment for me to focus on my pain.

I couldn't stop the tears. They kept coming. Burton handed me his handkerchief and whispered, "It's okay. Sometimes they're good tears and they need to be freed."

15

How could I have figured out what happened next? I want to be sure and get all the details right.

I was ready to say good night to Burton, go upstairs, and try to get some sleep. Shortly after I had opened up to Burton, the clock struck eleven.

"Are you sure you'll be all right?" he asked as we started out of the drawing room.

Before I could answer, we heard a gunshot followed by a scream. Both of us raced toward the stairway where the shot had come from. I didn't think of it then, but I outran him on the steps.

By the time I reached the landing, and Burton was two steps behind me, the others had come out of their rooms and stood in the hallway.

"I heard a shot!"

"And a scream."

"Is anyone hurt?"

I don't remember who said what, because everyone seemed to talk at once. All of them looked as if they had just jumped out of bed. Jason was the only one without a robe. He stood in jeans, bare feet, and bare chest.

Just then Wayne Holmestead poked his head out of his room, and the light was on behind him. His was the room at the end of the hallway.

When he saw us, he stumbled out of the room. He visibly shook. His glasses were askew. He slumped against the wall as if he feared he might fall. He seemed unable to move or to say anything.

Within seconds everyone focused on Wayne. He opened his mouth several times before words came out. "Somebody shot at me! I could — I could have been killed."

"Who shot at you?" Burton asked.

"I don't know."

He straightened his glasses and pushed himself away from the wall. He wore a robe over pajamas, and he tightened the belt. Those minor actions seemed to put him back in control. He stepped forward. "I had gone down the hallway and visited Paulette — perfectly innocent — just to borrow a Percodan — which I know she takes. I hadn't thought to bring any. I have an old football injury, and sometimes my sciatica acts up and the pain is excruciating. She gave me two pills, and I was returning to my room."

"There are the pills!" Lenny said, pointing. "So scared he dropped them, huh?"

We stared at the floor, and they were both on the carpet, about four feet apart from each other.

"Look! The door! Isn't that a bullet hole?" asked Reginald. He walked past Burton to the frame of the door. Embedded in the door was a bullet.

No one seemed to know enough about bullets to give any opinion about what kind of gun had been used.

Just then, Jason stepped forward and looked at the bullet lodged in the wood. Paulette hurriedly explained what had happened. Beth walked down to where Burton, Wayne, and I stood. She stared closely at the hole and the casing. "Beretta — .32 caliber," she said.

"How did you know that?" I asked.

"I know things like that."

"That's probably right," Jason said. "Because I think it's the gun from Dad's desk — we presume the one that killed him."

It took several seconds for all of us to absorb that information. I realized not only did we have two murders, but now we had an attempted third. What was going on here?

"Hey, sounds like the old Agatha Christie novel, *And Then There Were None.*" Lenny laughed. "You know the story? There were ten people on an island or an estate. One by one, they all died or something like that."

"Except the murderer killed himself, which made the last couple of people mistrust themselves and they killed each other," said Reginald. *"Or something like that."*

"That's so — so horrid," said Amanda. "Please. That's not something to joke about."

"I wasn't joking. Not this time," Lenny said and laughed. "Or maybe I was."

"Or maybe you have the gun?" Jeffery asked.

"Search me. Search my room," Lenny said. "Stay for tea in the morning."

"What do you think is going on?" I asked Burton. I kept my voice low, and most of them didn't hear me. By then, a gaggle of voices repeated to each other what they had heard, and most of them insisted they had been sleeping soundly.

"Are you afraid to be in your room alone?" Burton asked Wayne.

He shook his head. "I'm safe now, and I'll lock the door. I won't come out again until I hear others moving around in the hallway."

"I'll ring your room from the kitchen for breakfast," Amanda said. "As I said earlier, I'll have some kind of breakfast ready by 7:30."

Burton didn't tell anyone not to touch the bullet. In the TV shows, the hero always says that, and it always sounds stupid to me. Why would anyone want to touch it? Who wanted to feel a spent bullet in the door frame?

"Let's all go back to bed," Burton said. "Go inside, lock your doors. You'll be safe tonight."

"Aren't we going to search everyone's room?" asked Lenny. "That could be fun. I'd love to know what people brought into their rooms."

"Good night, Lenny," I said. "We'll leave that kind of thing to the police."

"Good night, everyone," Burton said. "I'll stand out in the hallway until everyone is locked inside."

The others turned and went into their rooms. That is everyone except me. I had been ready for bed, but now I was wide awake. I stared at Burton.

"I'm awake, too," he said. "You want to find some sweet tea or something downstairs?"

"I'd prefer a snack. If I eat something, that relaxes me."

We walked downstairs to the kitchen. Burton made himself an instant hot chocolate, and I found a box of Oreos. I planned to eat two but finished off eight without a pause. Burton just watched and smiled.

"I think I'm ready to head toward bed now," Burton said.

"Sounds like a good idea."

We left the kitchen and walked down the hallway. Just as we approached Roger Harden's office, I heard a soft, brushing noise — as if someone moved something inside the room. Burton paused. Our eyes met, and he put his index finger to his lips.

Burton turned the knob slowly and pushed open the door.

The lamp on Roger's desk was on. Paulette's back was to us, but she was rummaging through his desk. She was so focused on her search she didn't see or hear us. She lifted a pile of file folders from the right-hand drawer and skimmed them as if she wanted one particular paper.

"What are you searching for?" Burton asked.

Paulette jumped and gasped. Her hand went to her breast. "Oh, you startled me."

"You were so intent on your search, you never heard us," I said. "And obviously you haven't yet found what you want."

"So what papers are you looking for?" Burton asked. "They must be important to you."

"Yes, they are."

"How did you get in here?"

"Roger kept a spare key over the door ledge. He locked his office only when he had a party because he didn't want guests to wander in here accidentally." She forced herself to smile — and it was obvious it was forced — and added, "You know how it is with powerful men like Roger. They constantly fear someone will steal from them."

Burton held out his hand. "Why don't you give me the key? We can lock it behind us when we leave."

She handed him the key.

"What did you hope to find?" I asked.

"I'm not clever enough to think up a safe or evasive answer, so I think it's wiser if I say nothing." She pulled the top of her heavy hot-pink robe tighter around her neck. She may have been dressed for bed, but she hadn't taken off her makeup. I wondered what she wore under that robe.

"It might help us believe you didn't kill Roger if you tell us," Burton said as he walked closer to her. "If you don't tell us, it becomes easy to believe you killed him because he had something you wanted and wouldn't give it to you, so you shot him, and you came back to find it when you thought everyone had gone back to bed."

I walked over and pulled open her robe. She still wore the same black dress from earlier in the evening. "You haven't been to bed, have you?" I asked. I noticed her purse on the corner of the desk and decided to see if she had already taken anything.

She saw what I was going to do, and her hand reached the purse before I could touch it. "You may choose to believe whatever you wish." She opened her purse, fumbled around, and closed it angrily. "I forgot. I quit smoking two weeks ago." She laughed — a bit forced from my observation — and said, "Grabbing a cigarette was a nice way to give me a few seconds to collect my thoughts." She opened the purse again and shoved it toward me so I could look inside before she snapped it shut. "Satisfied?"

"Want to try a stick of gum instead?" Burton held out a pack.

She shook her head.

I couldn't understand how she could search through Roger's desk when his body lay on the floor less than two feet away. *What kind of woman is she?* I wondered.

From behind the desk she had carelessly tossed file folders around. Burton came around on one side of the desk to face her, and I came around from the other — the side away from the covered corpse. Without discussing it, I sensed both of us wanted her to feel intimidated by our presence.

She stared at me and then at Burton but said nothing. She sat down in Roger's chair. Her face was a mask and she wasn't going to reveal anything.

"You disliked Roger, didn't you?" I asked.

"Disliked him? I *loathed* him." She laughed. "But I'm not a murderer, even though I'm glad someone took care of him."

"Why did you loathe him?" Burton asked.

"Let's just leave the statement at that, shall we? You're not a police officer, so I don't have to answer, do I?"

Burton sat on the edge of the desk, and he invaded her space just enough to intimidate her. "You're right, of course; however, I'd like to leave this office believing that you're not the cold-blooded killer who's already taken two lives. You don't have to say anything."

"Do you think I killed Roger? Do you honestly believe that?"

"What do you want me to think?" As Burton talked to her, his voice softened and took on a kind of intimate confidentiality. An act or not, if Burton had talked to me like that, I would have spilled every secret I had ever learned.

"Let's just say I had no love for him or even that I detested him. Now that he's gone, I haven't shed any tears, and I won't. I think the world is better without Roger. I feel sad about Elaine. I didn't particularly like her, but she didn't deserve to die."

"And you have some way to know who deserves death?" I asked. "You are some kind of judge?"

"No, I didn't mean —"

"What did you mean?" I reached down, pulled the chair around so she faced me. I grabbed her shoulders. Burton had tried the let's-be-sweet approach. Now I would try mine. I shook her twice. "Don't try to play games with us. Someone has killed two people and shot at a third. If you didn't kill them, I would expect you to do everything you can to turn suspicion away from yourself."

"Take your hands off me."

Her words lacked conviction. I didn't shake her again, but I didn't let go. I had suspected that, although she was cool on the outside, she was fragile on the inside. "Then tell us."

"I want to be able to believe you," Burton said in his still-soft voice.

"Is this some kind of good-cop-bad-cop deal?" Her voice shook as she asked.

I knew we had her.

"I wouldn't play games with you," Burton said. If anyone else had used those words, I would have cried, "Yuck," but they came across with sincerity. "Please."

I released her and stepped back. I pushed the file drawers back into place and sat down on the other side of the desk.

Paulette swiveled her chair back so that she faced Burton. She closed her eyes and leaned her head back in the chair. "I'm too ashamed to talk about it."

"Please tell us," Burton said. "We're both professionals, and we'll respect your confidence."

Paulette opened her deep blue eyes. "Is that a promise?" She didn't look at me. Her full concentration was on Burton. I suspected that was part of her charm in the business world. She stared at him as if he were the only person in the room.

This time I was smart enough to keep my mouth closed. Burton was doing a good job, and I was willing to let him do it.

16

"Roger Harden was my mentor," Paulette said without looking at either of us.

"And you loved him and he was your best friend," I said. "We read that novel. Now let's try a little nonfiction."

She nodded two or three times as if trying to decide where to start. "We met when I was nineteen years old and struggling to finish my degree in business at the University of Tennessee — in Knoxville — and I worked full-time at Faces."

"What's Faces?" Burton asked.

"It was a high-level cosmetics firm. It was fairly small by industry standards, but they made only quality products — not the kind you find in Walgreens or Kmart. I was in sales. I mean, I spoke only to top buyers — Macy's, Nordstrom — that kind of place. We had a few independent stores, but mostly it was the upper-end chains. Apparently, I was extremely good at what I did, because week after week I brought in the top sales for Faces, and there were eleven salespeople on staff."

"And how did Roger discover your talent?"

"Oh that? He decided to buy the company. We were located just outside of Knoxville, and he wanted to take us over, move us down here to the coast, and make Faces a megabucks outfit — or so he said."

"I didn't realize Roger was into anything like that."

"Roger was into whatever would make him a profit. He bought Faces, reorganized it, brought in top talent, and made the company big — really big — and six months later he sold it to Bristol-Myers. They downgraded the products — cheapened them, if you want my opinion. But Roger didn't care what they did as long as he made a profit. In the process, he netted a few million and moved on to the next project. That's how he operated."

"And how did you fit into all of that?"

"Simple. Roger was brilliant. Anyone will tell you that. He had an intuitive instinct about him. It was almost as if he looked at a product or a line — even if he knew nothing about it — and could sense what would sell and what wouldn't. He was the same way about people. In the twenty years I was with Roger, not once did I ever see him make a bad deal. He was that good."

"I'm still not clear —" I said and remembered I was supposed to keep my mouth shut.

"Roger knew I had potential. He spotted it within minutes of our meeting the first time he came to Faces. Privately, he asked me if I would meet him for lunch — strictly business, he said. But I had classes at the university, so we settled on dinner. That night he offered to make me a vice president — one of four in Harden Enterprises."

"Just like that?" I said, and I admit skepticism rang out in my voice.

"Just like that. He said he would give me flextime to finish my degree — which he did. He even backed me so I could do an MBA. In those regards, Roger was the best."

"And in other ways?" I prompted. As I asked, Burton raised an eyebrow. I caught the message. I'd try to keep my mouth shut.

"Roger taught me many things, and always he acted as a man of discreet conduct —"

"You mean he didn't make a pass at you?" I said and wondered if I needed to literally bite my tongue.

"Never. He was a total professional. I knew he was married — he married a few months after I started to work for him. You can believe this: No matter what a jerk he was, it was always business. Totally, strictly business. No, Roger was one of those people for whom the ultimate aphrodisiac was money, which meant success, and success meant power."

I had a comment ready, but this time I said nothing.

"I loved my work with Roger — at least I did for the first ten years. I learned more on the job and from him than I ever could have learned on my own." She paused and smiled. "Both Harvard and Princeton offered me a teaching position last year — which I turned down. But that's to make it clear how much Roger taught me, and to explain that I had become well-known for my business sense."

"But you despised him?" I said softly. This time Burton didn't raise an eyebrow.

"He did teach me — I received a great education from him, but that instruction came at a price. Roger would coach me or open any doors I wanted to go through. There was just one catch."

"Total control," I said without thinking.

"Exactly that. I had to turn down Harvard and Princeton because I would be too far away from him. Everything, anything —

it didn't matter what it was — Roger Harden had to be in total control." She shook her head, swiveled in her chair several seconds. "He liked my ideas — that was never a problem. But I had to bring every idea and every innovation to him. No matter what, it was as if he had to put his imprimatur on it."

"But you said he liked your ideas?"

"He never rejected one of them. Two or three times he made suggestions to improve the concepts or figured out ways for me to get more mileage, but that's all. I didn't mind that, and he never demanded credit. He didn't seem to want that kind of power. It wasn't anything like that."

"But it was the control issue, right?" I asked.

She nodded. "If I didn't consult him on every single thing, he would go berserk. One time he yelled at me for almost twenty minutes in a board meeting. Do you know why? Because I had forgotten to hand deliver to him a copy of our profit-and-loss statement — and we had netted nearly three million dollars. *Hand deliver.* Can you imagine that? I sent it by the office messenger because I was running late for an appointment."

"That must have been demeaning," Burton said.

"Demeaning? You have no idea. Another time I hired a secretary. An entry-level secretary! But I didn't tell Roger first. He was angry because I didn't tell him that I had interviewed four candidates, liked her the best, and offered the position. He made me fire her. Is that micro-micromanagement or what? I don't know how he kept all that going inside his head, because I know I wasn't the only one. Even though I realized he was that way with everyone under his powerful hand, I didn't feel any better."

"It must have worn on you," I said.

"Worn on me? Ha! That's understated. It grated on me every day — every day. I kept reminding myself that I was making a lot of money because of Roger. He also taught me how to invest wisely — which I've done."

"So where does the hate come in?" Burton asked. "He could have been a nuisance, but —"

"He lost interest in my career. It was as if I had become a finished product. He had taken me, molded me, and made me what he wanted me to be. Then he had no further interest in me. I still had to drive through his control booth, but there was a tone of disdain."

"Disdain? I'm not sure what you mean,"

Burton said.

"He began to make me feel insignificant and reminded me constantly that whatever I was, he had made me. Things like that. He said I would have been nothing without his guidance. And he sometimes said those things in board meetings or whenever important people were around."

"So what did you do?" I asked. "You don't seem like the kind of woman who would just take that forever." I'm sure she knew I hinted that she might have hated him enough to kill him.

"I suggested to him that I leave and move elsewhere. He went into a tirade over that. He screamed at me and called me ungrateful. That night he phoned me just before midnight and again called me an ingrate and self-centered and said I had only wanted to use him for my own means."

"And what did you say?" Burton asked.

"I said, 'If I'm so terrible, then perhaps it is better if I leave.' Then he really screamed and finally said, 'You will leave Harden Enterprises *only* when I tell you to leave. If you try to apply for another position, I'll ruin you!' "

I reached over, took Paulette's hand, and squeezed it gently. I knew enough about Roger that I could understand her feelings.

I hadn't liked her before. I still didn't like her, but at least I understood her pain.

Burton and I didn't say anything more. Both of us seemed to sense if we just kept quiet, she would open up.

"Okay. I'll tell you. You're both professionals, right?"

We nodded.

"That means whatever I say to you is confidential? Burton's clergy and you're a therapist. You assure me of confidentiality, and I'll tell you."

We both assured her that we would hold everything in confidence unless she gave us permission to speak.

The words poured out. She worked most of the years for a subsidiary of Harden Enterprises, but her offices were in Roger's twelve-story office building. "I was in charge of a chemical company that wanted to develop a natural insecticide that would not harm the environment." She knew nothing about the formula, but she stood behind All-Well Chemicals as they developed their product. They spent millions of dollars, and after three years, they reached the final stages of development. They would have to test its effectiveness — especially the long-term effects, then they would be able to put it on the market within two years.

A friend had invited Paulette to a cocktail party. One of the other guests was the CEO of a rival firm. The CEO said he had asked the friend to invite Paulette because he wanted to offer her a job. She would become acting president and succeed him in five years. He was willing to write a contract. When she told them that Roger would try to block it, he promised a contract that would prevent the company from firing her. If they did release her, they would give her a five-million-dollar bonus for every year she worked there.

"It was too good an offer to pass up," she said, "but there was just one problem."

"And that was?" I asked.

"I had to steal the formula from All-Well Chemicals and pass it on. Oh, they would make small changes so that it wouldn't be exactly the same. They were working toward the same goal, and it would have saved them millions in research."

"Did you have any qualms?"

"Not really. That sort of industrial espionage goes on all the time. I also convinced myself that it was my way to get even with Roger for his years of dominance."

"So you went through with it?" Burton prompted.

"I was so filled with disgust for Roger, I

said yes without even taking time to think it over." Within a week she had copied the formula and had done it so that no one could prove she had stolen it.

"The day before I was to deliver the formula, Roger called me into his office. 'Where is the formula?' he demanded. 'I want your copy of it.' I didn't try to argue with him. I have no idea how he found out I had copied it. I had simply downloaded it onto a flash drive. I took the flash drive out of my purse and handed it to him.

"He didn't fire me, and he wouldn't let me resign. He didn't yell or say anything, but the smirk on his face said, 'I know everything you do.' He finally said, 'I told you that you would stay here as long as I want you here. I choose to keep you here. For now.' "

"That was the end of it?" Burton asked.

"Almost. He sent me a memo the next morning — a memo, mind you — in a sealed envelope. His secretary brought it to me and said Roger had instructed her to wait for a response.

"He sent my confession. He stated that I was to sign it because it was industrial theft, after all — and it could send me to jail. He *instructed* me — I mean that. He spelled it all out and even numbered the paragraphs.

The final item, number 6, told me to sign the confession. Then he stated that I was not to date it. That way, whether it was one year or ten — despite the statute of limitations — he had control.

"You want to know something else? He knew about the cocktail party. He knew everything. I have no idea how he got all that information, but he had it, and it was totally accurate."

"You think he set you up?" I asked.

"I don't think so, because he also had a second paper for me to sign — and that one I dated. That was to turn down the other position 'for the sake of my own conscience.' I'm sure Roger loved writing that statement."

Burton said nothing, but his eyes told both of us that he understood.

She nodded slowly, and I think she was pushing back the urge to cry. "He had it all figured out. He had me tied up for as long as he wanted me."

"Now you're searching for the confession, is that it?" I asked.

"Yes, and I have no idea where it is. I can't find it among his papers, and I know he would never leave it at the business office."

"So you figured —" I said.

"It had to be here. Where else could it be?

But it's not here. I've been through everything twice. I'm now convinced it's not in this office unless he has some secret compartment." She sank back into the chair. "I hardly saw him this past year. In fact, it was quite a relief. I sent him everything by our interoffice e-mail or by messenger, because that was how he wanted it — no more face-to-face contact. Then I received the invitation — the summons — and I came." She leaned forward. "I am ambitious — ambitious enough to be a thief — but not ambitious enough to take someone's life."

I wanted to say, "I believe you," but what if she was fooling me? What if she had killed Roger? What if Mrs. Wright had seen her, and Paulette had decided to get rid of the only witness? Instead of saying anything, I gave her a quick pat on the shoulder. I had no idea how truthful she was, but she certainly had plenty of motive to kill Roger Harden.

17

We asked Paulette to put everything back where it belonged and she started to do that as we left. I didn't think to say anything to her about fingerprints. Or maybe it's only in movies that detectives check those things.

Burton and I left, went into the hall, and headed back toward the kitchen. "I need another Oreo," I said. It was now almost midnight, and I had begun to feel tired. I confess that I liked being with Burton and felt we had already developed a camaraderie. I still thought he was good-looking, and now that I had seen him in operation with people, I liked him even more as a professional.

I also liked the fact that he didn't try to convert me to his religion. I once dated a man who did. Every time there was the slightest opportunity, he'd insert some comment about my need for God. When I resisted, he'd tell me that unless I heeded and believed, I'd go to hell. "Listen," I finally said, "I don't know anything about hell, but that's what you're making life for me right now, so cut it out. You asked for a date, and this isn't any preaching meeting. If you invited me to dinner to convert me, the price is too high."

I smile about that experience. We were sitting in a restaurant and had nearly finished the meal when I spoke up. He got up, threw his napkin on the table, and said, "I hope you enjoy your torment in hell, because it will last a long time." The jerk didn't even pick up the check. So I had to buy his dinner as well as endure his lecture most of the evening.

Burton was different — I still waited for his religion pitch — they all have it. I was sure that's why they go to seminary. Even when I opened up to him, he didn't tell me what a horrible sinner I was. But I knew he would.

They all did.

Once we were inside the kitchen, without asking, Burton plugged in the coffee machine and measured the water and the grounds. I accommodated him by putting out two cups and saucers.

"Oh, I thought I was the only one who couldn't sleep," Amanda Harden said as she walked into the kitchen. Even in her robed pajamas, she still looked attractive. I sure hoped that at her age — which must be fifty or more — I'd look that good at 12:02 in the morning.

"We couldn't sleep," Burton said. "In fact, neither of us has tried."

"Can you tell us anything?" I asked her. I pulled another cup and saucer from the cupboard. "You were Roger's wife. Surely you either know or suspect something."

She sat down on a chair. It was a large kitchen and held a table that seated twelve people — which made it larger than my dining room and kitchen combined. That was Roger. He liked everything big.

"I've thought a great deal about him this evening," she said. "I did love Roger in the beginning — and I think I made that clear — but the more I saw of who he was, the more I pulled away from him. He bought me expensive gifts — jewelry, furs, and cars — you know — things and only expensive things. He offered to set me up with any kind of business I wanted. He knew I had money and didn't need anything, but he loved to tell me how much richer he was than I was and how he had increased his wealth. He also reminded me that although I had inherited mine, he had earned his money. He used to quote that old TV commercial about getting money the old-fashioned way. 'I earn it.' I never could make him understand that I didn't want more money or homes. We own homes in six different parts of the world. Can you believe that?"

"Six? That's a lot," I said.

"I wanted a normal relationship with him. I wanted to be his companion, not his slave."

"Yes, I think we understood that," I said. "Anything else?"

"I'm not sure what to make of this — and that's why I couldn't sleep. Roger changed. I'm not sure when. Maybe two months ago. He became moody — and he was never moody before. One time — oh, maybe a week before I left him — he stood and seemed to stare at the cliff — the place where we dock. I was weeding flowers, and he didn't know I was around. He cried out, 'What's wrong with me? What's wrong with me?'

"I ducked down behind the peonies and rhododendrons until he left. He turned and faced the ocean. He screamed other words, but I couldn't hear them. He was there maybe ten minutes. Then he turned and walked back toward the house. He never glanced my way, and I never told him I had heard him. But that was such a shock. Never had I ever heard Roger entertain the thought that something was wrong with *him*."

The aroma of coffee had begun to waft through the kitchen. I also became aware that I was hungry. I opened the refrigerator, found a foil-wrapped plate of sandwiches, pulled out the plate, and unwrapped them. I took a cheese-on-rye and offered the plate to Burton and Amanda.

"Elaine made those. She was so thoughtful and always made them for late-night snacks." She stopped and wiped tears from her face. "I didn't like her very much, but I'm sorry she's dead. I didn't know about the robbery, but that certainly explains to me why she was often curt."

Burton poured coffee. He picked up an egg-salad sandwich and munched on it. "Hmm, this is good," he said. "Homemade bread. I don't get that often."

For several minutes the conversation went boring. I don't cook, and I don't like to talk about food. I try to patronize restaurants to keep the economy booming — and I certainly do my part to keep Americans gainfully employed.

"There was one other thing," Amanda said. She laid aside her half-eaten tuna-with-Swiss sandwich. "One time Roger and

Simon were having a heated discussion. It may have been an argument, but it didn't sound angry — loud, strong, but not angry. Something about a book. Simon said, 'You don't have to *like* the book.' He held up a book — I could see that much. Roger yelled something back — something like, 'I don't like it, and I don't have to like it, and I refuse to like it.' "

"I'll bet Simon shrugged," I said.

"Correct. He put the book into a briefcase and started to walk away. He did stop, turn around, and say, 'But if you decide you want to read it, I have two copies.' "

"Sounds interesting," Burton said, "but I'm not sure how relevant that is."

"What is relevant is this. First, Simon spoke in full sentences. I had never heard him speak that way before — he had fooled me the way he did everyone else. Second, and this is the main thing, Simon spoke to him frankly, even strongly, and Roger didn't scream. I'd observed Roger when he screamed at Simon in the past — many times — and always over trivial things. That's what makes this so odd. Roger smiled after he said he didn't like the book. *He truly smiled.* In eighteen years of marriage, I never once saw Roger smile when someone talked strongly to him. And Simon was an employee, which made it worse. Or at least it was strange."

"Perhaps we need to talk to Simon," I said.

"That wouldn't hurt," Burton said and reached for another sandwich.

Amanda tried the phone. "Still out." She finished her coffee, threw the uneaten part of her sandwich into the garbage can, and said good night to us.

Burton quietly munched his second sandwich. I knew he wanted to go to bed. I needed the sleep, but I could always catch up on sleep, and I wanted to prolong our time together. I liked this guy. Just being around him made me feel better about myself.

I sat quietly and wondered how many people made me feel good about myself just being with them. I had a friend named Nan Snipes. She does that for me, but I couldn't think of anyone else.

"What are you thinking about?" he asked.

I know I blushed, so I said, "About you." Before he could respond, I said, "You're the first preacher I ever met who didn't start every fifth sentence with some reference to God."

"I'd love to talk to you about God — if you want and when you want."

I laughed, but I'm sure he knew I was

embarrassed. "I'm not very tactful, am I?"

"No, but I like your directness. It's real."

"So I suppose almost everybody brings up God even if you don't."

"Most of the time. They either tell me some of their best friends are preachers or that they were forced to go to Sunday school and hated it. Sometimes they'll say, 'I haven't been inside a church in twenty years.' "

"How do you respond to that?"

"Come on back," I say. "God's still waiting to hear from you, and it's about time to visit again." He laughed. "No, I don't say that. I usually ask them why. Most of the time, they're open enough to tell me. I understand why a lot of people have turned away from the church. I just wish they wouldn't turn away from God, as well."

"Interesting perspective," I said. "I never thought of distinguishing the two."

"Think about it. The church means people — and all of us are flawed. God is the perfect One. That's the direction I like to point people — from imperfect people to a perfect God."

"Makes sense. Yes, one way or another, if they're around you long enough, everyone does gets around to the topic of God with you priests."

"Pastor. Not a priest. I'm a Protestant."
He grinned. "But you knew that, didn't
you?"

I laughed. I was doing a little harmless
playing — the dumb-girl act and probably a
little flirting. I didn't think a pastor-type
would be interested in me, but then, I loved
his curls and nice smile. He was the most
attractive man and the nicest I'd met in at
least two years. Okay, he was maybe half an
inch shorter than I am, but no one is perfect.

"You don't act like a preacher — at least
not the kind I was exposed to as a kid."

"Maybe it's time to be exposed to a new
type."

He looked directly into my eyes when he
said those words. *That's not fair,* I wanted to
say. *I'm trying to flirt and you're getting serious.* "Uh, well, maybe. Right now I'm trying to get a few things straight in my life —
my boring life."

"I'm sure it's not boring," he said, but he
continued to focus his total attention on
me. "Have you tried God?" he asked quietly.
The words were spoken so softly I wondered
if I had imagined them.

"Not yet, but I'm running out of options."

"God may be your best option and not
just your last one."

"If a belief in God helps you, by all means,

206

you need to believe it or practice it or whatever you tell people to do."

"Belief is a good place to start."

This conversation wasn't going the way I wanted. I needed to switch topics. "You make it easy to talk. And you're pretty funny."

"You're pretty. Period."

"I didn't know preachers had a sense of humor."

"It comes from arguing with nonbelieving redheads." He smiled before he said, "We preacher-types work on it. I took a course in seminary called Laugh 101. I was the only student."

That was a silly remark, but he said it with such a serious voice, in spite of myself, I laughed.

Just then I thought of something.

"I have no idea why I thought of this now, but Roger phoned me twice. Oh, it's been a month or more since he called. We talked about general things, mostly about my workload. It was something he said just before I was ready to hang up. At the time I thought it was odd, but now it seems even odder."

"What did he say?"

"He asked me if I ever thought about religion. Did I think God had forgiven me for the accident?"

"And you said?"

"You know me. I'm the smart mouth. So I said, 'I have no idea. Since God and I have never been introduced, we haven't discussed it.' "

" 'But if you did talk about it,' he persisted. 'Think about it.' I did think about it, and I told him I thought the topic was irrelevant. I tried that old line that God stays out of my business and I stay out of his."

"Did he say anything else?"

I closed my eyes and concentrated. "Let's see, that was the first time. No, he didn't. He just said good night. Maybe two weeks later he called again."

"Julie, do you remember our last conversation?" Roger said. "I asked you if you thought God would forgive you. I wanted you to think about it. So, what do you think?"

"I don't know. Why do you ask?"

"No big reason —"

"Sure it is, or you wouldn't have brought it up. What's going on?"

"Nothing really," he said. "I went to church last week —"

"To church? You?"

"It would take too long to explain the

reason, but yes, I did. Since then, I've been wondering about a few things. That's all. So how do you feel about being forgiven?"

"How would I know? That's totally outside my experience."

"Yes, I suppose it is," he said quietly and after a pause added, "totally outside mine, as well."

"Are you turning religious?"

"I certainly hope not," he said. He laughed — more of a sneer. "The speaker at church made several provocative statements. I have never talked to anyone before who could say he or she felt forgiven by God. So it was merely a topic of passing interest."

I had kept my eyes closed — somehow it seemed to make it easier to remember. I opened them and said, "Just one thing about that conversation bothered me — which is probably why I remembered."

"What was that?" Burton asked.

"His final words before he said good-bye. He said it was merely a topic of passing interest. But the tone of his voice — something about the way he said it — made me know that it was more than something of passing interest."

"What do you think?"

"After all this? My guess is that Roger

Harden may have developed a conscience."

"In what way?"

"I don't know, but I suspect he called us here to confront us and to expose us to each other. Maybe it was to tell us that he was going to turn over everything to the police."

"Could be," he said. "I do think one thing is now obvious. All the guests have something to hide — something Roger had on them — something wrong or unlawful."

"Is that true with you?" I asked.

"I came because of Jason. Remember?"

"I remember that's what Jason *thought.*"

"Or perhaps he wanted to confess his wrongdoings."

"Do you think that's possible?"

Burton smiled. "As we Christian types say, 'anything is possible with God.' "

"I'm not sure God had anything to do with it."

18

My name is Dr. James Burton, but no one calls me James. I'm just Burton to everyone. Julie said she was going to write down everything that happened on Palm Island. She won't allow me to see it. She says it's her secret diary, but she wants to make sure we won't forget anything.

I'm not a writer, and I avoid writing whenever I can. But as a favor to Julie, I agreed to write this part. There is a segment of the story where she wasn't involved. So I'll tell it from my perspective.

Before I tell my part of the story, I want to point out that I like Julie. She's refreshing. We have a big gulf between us, so I don't see anything romantic happening. I was aware of her flirting — her frequent flirting. It's flattering, even though she now realizes that it won't lead anywhere. She's certainly not like that tarantula type I run into — they grab hold and keep after me.

It's nice to know she finds me attractive enough to flirt with. Like that thing about her tripping on the path. I wonder how many times females have tried that one on me. It goes all the way back to tenth grade when Jennifer Schuchmann tried it on me the first time.

As much as I like Julie, however, we don't have enough commonality. My faith is too important to compromise. I'm not sure she understands that because faith doesn't mean anything to her. That's the big problem.

That's really too bad. I like her.

Julie and I talked in the kitchen for a few minutes and I began to yawn. Then she yawned. I yawned again, and she tried to make more noise with her yawn than I did.

"Enough. Let's go to our rooms," I said.

We walked upstairs, and I waited in the hallway until she opened her door.

"You're really gallant," she said. She stepped inside, and just before she closed the door, she smiled and said, "Thanks for being nice to this heathen."

I wanted to reply, but she closed the door.

I fell across the bed and didn't even bother to undress. I must have dozed, because something awakened me. I wasn't sure what it was, but I was instantly alert. I got out of bed, crept to the door, and opened it. I didn't see anyone in the hallway, but I had the distinct sense that someone had passed my door. It was the last room before the stairs.

I peeked into the hallway, but I didn't see anyone. I closed my door silently and left my room. On the stairway I saw nothing. I crept silently down the dark steps. Before I reached the bottom, I spotted a light from under Roger's office door.

Does everybody have a key to that office? I asked myself.

I turned the knob slowly. As I did so, I wondered if the intruder had a gun. That was a chance I'd have to take. As I pushed the door forward a fraction of an inch at a time, I peered inside.

Jason had pulled out the same files that Paulette had gone through. He did it differently. He took out the drawer itself and laid it on the desk and then pulled out the files one at a time. He was so focused on the files he didn't notice me.

"What are you doing?" I asked.

A startled Jason dropped the manila file folder. Several sheets of paper fluttered to the floor. He dropped to his knees and picked them up.

"Looking. Just looking for — for something."

I didn't want to make this difficult for Jason, so I sat down on the sofa across from the desk. "I can see that."

"You don't think I killed him, do you? I wouldn't do that — I couldn't kill anyone — not Dad, especially not now."

The best way to handle Jason was to say as little as possible. He had become active in our congregation, and I had gotten to know him fairly well.

"I know this looks so totally bad for me — like the murderer coming back to the scene of the crime, like he wanted to pick up the one piece of evidence that would, like, convict him."

"Is that what's going on?"

"Oh no. It — well, it just looks so totally that way, don't you think?"

"You certainly think that way."

"I was, uh, like, looking for something — I mean like something Dad had earlier — earlier, like when I saw him before tea."

Whenever Jason resorted to the frequent use of *like,* I could tell he was rattled. He used to say that *like* and *so totally* were part of his school style, but when he spoke with adults, he normally used an adult vocabulary.

I stuck my hands in my pockets, sat still, and smiled at him.

He laughed. "You used to do that in your office. Just like that."

"I know."

"So — is this, uh, like, some kind of counseling session?"

"Is that what you want it to be?"

"Can it be?"

"If you like."

"Okay, I'll tell you."

I knew he would. Jason is a good kid. He's amazingly mature at times, but once in a while he acts as if he's thirteen. I like the boy. Despite moments of immaturity, he's solid. His struggles with Roger Harden haven't been easy.

"It was something Dad wanted to read to us — right after dinner. That's what I'm searching for."

"What was it?"

"I don't know."

"Any idea?"

"A list of all our sins maybe? I don't know, but that's what I think. You know, Mr. Burton, every person in that room had something to hide — something bad they did and Dad found out. I don't know all of them, but I know he held something over their heads."

"So what was he going to do? Read his own emancipation proclamation? Or threaten to call the police?"

"I don't know. He was well, like acting so totally weird. I mean, yeah, weird. I can't think of another way to say it."

"In what way was he weird? I mean, you haven't told me enough to make me understand."

"You know a lot of the story," he said and sat down on the far end of the sofa from me, near enough for him to feel close but far enough that he would know this was a counseling session.

I did know a lot of his story. Jason's birth father died when he was only a baby, so he really has no memories of the man. Amanda married Roger when Jason was about two years old, which made Roger the only male parent the boy had ever known. His step-father didn't understand children — even he admitted that to Jason. He tried to treat the boy like an employee. He never spent time with his stepson or encouraged him. Jason often complained that he wouldn't attend any of his basketball or baseball games.

"If he didn't grumble over the grades on my report card," Jason once said, "that was his way of giving me approval. If I made a lower grade than he thought I should have, then I'd get The Big Lecture on how to study."

I felt sorry for the boy. He studied hard, and I knew that. Several times he had come to see me at my office, and he brought his laptop and school books. If he arrived ten minutes early, he used those minutes to study — and it wasn't to impress me. He was just that self-disciplined about his studies. Two of Jason's teachers were members of our congregation. Both said he studied hard, was extremely bright, and never handed in late papers.

The only complaint I ever heard about him was that he tended to be moody. Later I learned that whenever he endured The Big Lecture from Roger, he would feel depressed for two or three days.

As I stared at the boy with his clean-cut American good looks, I thought what a shame it was that he had had to go through so much.

"You taught me something important, Mr. Burton," Jason said.

"Really? What's that?"

"You were — and still are — the best father figure in my life. You're the kind of dad I wished I had."

I hardly knew what to say to him. I had been aware, of course, that Jason liked me, but I had no idea I had become that important to him.

"Remember how you used to walk me to the door of your office and give me a hug?"

"Sure. I do that —" I stopped because I started to say I did it with most people I knew fairly well.

"I'd always close my eyes and think, *This is the way a dad's hug should feel.* Whenever I visited your office, you always made me feel better."

"I had no idea —"

"Yeah, I know. That's why I like you. You weren't trying to be a dad. You were just being who you are."

I felt slightly uncomfortable. I liked Jason, but I wasn't used to having the conversation focused on me. I cleared my throat and asked, "So tell me what happened after you came back to the coast." He had studied two years at Clayton University even though Roger and Amanda had moved permanently to Palm Island.

"As you know, I transferred to Georgia Southern in Statesboro this past year. Dad asked me to do that. No, he told me — he commanded it. He said that if I wasn't going to attend one of the best schools in the country, at least I could study fairly close to home. He wanted me home on weekends."

"Did you come home?"

"When I had to and when I couldn't work out an excuse to stay over."

"It must have been hard for you to come home like that."

"Yes, it was — until maybe a month ago. That's when things changed. That's when Dad changed."

I must have leaned forward, because Jason chuckled. "Now I know you're listening carefully. Whenever you do that, I know you're hanging on to every word."

I probably blushed then — and people tell me I do a good blush. This was one observant kid.

"You like me and you helped me — most of all you helped me. I went to another shrink — you didn't know that, but I had to because Dad made me. The guy was a good shrink, but he never did dig what made me the way I am. No matter how much I talked, he always kept telling me that I had to forgive myself. Like all I had to do was say, 'I forgive myself.' I just wanted to forgive Dad. That was until you helped me turn to the Lord and ask God to forgive me. And because of your help, I was able to forgive Dad — not right away — but eventually."

"Do you realize you never called him Dad before last night? At least not with me?" I had noticed that earlier. He was always Roger.

"He became my dad — he wasn't good at it — but he tried."

As I waited for Jason to continue, I became aware that the rain had softened from earlier in the evening. It was as if the clouds were running out of moisture.

"Dad did change — not a lot — but he was, well, different. At least he was different toward me. He still yelled, and I heard him really give it to ol' Holmestead one day on the phone. He used words he would have whacked me across the face for if he'd heard me say them."

"How did he change toward you?"

Jason stared into space. "Mostly, he was quieter, I think. Yeah, that's how it started. He didn't pick on me all the time. My grades were all good, but in the past, he'd still find something to diss me about."

"You're convinced that he changed and not you?"

"Oh, I changed, too. Maybe that's what started it. You helped me a lot there. You kept urging me to accept him as he was — and not wait until he became a good father to me. That was hard, but I did. You told me to pray for him every day."

I remembered that time very well. I had

suggested to Jason that instead of trying to change his father, he might pray for himself — pray that he would be able to accept and love his stepfather. If he could love his stepfather, he could accept Roger's imperfections. Jason told me that he would pray for Roger at least once a day. I also know that a year later, he said he still prayed.

"I told you the others had a secret — something wrong they did," Jason said.

"Yes, you did."

"I did, too. I'm not here just because I'm his stepson. I — I did something wrong — really wrong."

"Want to tell me about it?" I hated using those words because that's a standard phrase in counseling, but I meant them.

"It started with a phone call on a Thursday evening. Dad said, 'I want you home by four o'clock tomorrow.' When I asked him why, he said, 'You'll find out when I tell you. Just be here.' "

"Did you know why he wanted you home?"

He nodded. "I would have had to be stupid not to know. Do you remember one time you read from someplace in the Bible where it said, 'Be sure your sin will find you out'?"

I didn't remember quoting the verse, but

that wasn't the point.

"My sin sure found me out. About five months ago, I forged his name on personal checks. I stole a book of his checks from his desk." He shook his head slowly. "I didn't need the money. I was just mad. I wanted to do something to hurt him. I ordered dumb stuff to be delivered to his office — you know, stuff from Victoria's Secret — really dumb things — and I paid for them with his forged checks."

"Didn't you know he'd catch you?"

"If I had stopped to reason it out, sure. I was so filled with anger I wanted to do something to — to get even — to make him really as angry as I was."

"Was there something in particular?"

"I turned twenty. He hadn't remembered my birthday — but then, he hadn't remembered my nineteenth, either. I was trying hard to forgive him and —" Jason's tears stopped him from saying anything more.

I moved over and put my arm around Jason and let him cry. I wasn't sure why he needed to cry, but I sensed he needed me to understand and to care.

"I always thought he hated me," Jason finally said.

"Do you still think so?"

"I — I need to find that paper — that

paper he planned to read. Then I'll know for sure how he felt."

19

Jason's body convulsed with tears. "I was wrong. Really wrong. And stupid."

I held him until the tears subsided. The rain had definitely passed. Now the aftermath of the storm threw all its energy into wind. The house creaked. Trees banged against the side of the house, but I heard no rain.

"See, when I came home, I was ready to get The Big Lecture — and I assumed he'd give me another on ethical and moral behavior."

Jason lapsed into silence again. When he spoke, he told me what had happened Friday afternoon, before the rest of us arrived.

"Come into my office, young man," Roger ordered. "Sit down." Jason started to say something, and Roger said, "Shut up and listen."

Jason had prepared himself for the worst possible consequences. The worst would be if his stepfather told him to leave the house and never come back. He didn't care if the old man cut off his allowance. He had saved money, and his mother had her own money. He couldn't think of a really bad thing Roger could do that would hurt him.

Jason sat stiffly in front of the desk, his head bowed. He listened without response and stared at his watch as the seconds ticked by. He always surreptitiously checked the time whenever Roger lectured. So far, the old man's record had been twenty-three minutes and eight seconds. He expected to hit thirty minutes today.

"I'm ashamed of you," Roger said. "Very ashamed."

Jason looked up briefly, made his face look extremely contrite, and bowed his head again. He considered whether to fake a few tears.

"I'm more ashamed of myself than I am of you," Roger said. "You are a good boy — an extremely good boy. I have failed you."

Jason waited. He knew Roger wouldn't say, "I'm sorry," because those words weren't part of his vocabulary; however, he figured this was as close as it would ever get.

"I assume this was some kind of payback. I deserved this kind of treatment."

Jason's head jerked up and he stared at his stepfather.

He wanted to hate the man, wanted to tell him how rotten he had been through the years, how cold and indifferent he had always been. Instead, he said, "I'm sorry."

Roger held up his hand. "Let's say no more about this, but I'd appreciate it if you would return the checks you haven't used." He smiled at Jason. "I'm going to try to be a real father to you. It's not exactly my strong suit, but I intend to try."

"That is a great start," Jason said, not knowing what else to say. Then he did something he had never done before: He grabbed his stepfather and hugged him. It felt as if he had hugged a marble statue, but Jason didn't let go.

Roger finally relaxed — slightly. He didn't pull away, so Jason held him for a long time. When he finally let go, he whispered to his stepfather, "Thank you."

Roger shook his hand, and Jason grinned. "It's a beginning."

"There are things we need to talk about," Roger said. He held up a folder with a number of sheets of paper tucked inside. "I was going to save this until tonight when everyone is here, but maybe you need to see it first."

"What is it?"

Just then, Wayne Holmestead knocked on the door and pushed it open. Without being invited inside — something Jason had never seen anyone else do — Holmestead said, "We need to talk."

"I'll be free in a few minutes," Roger said.

"This can't wait. We need to talk. *Now.*"

Roger patted Jason's shoulder. "We'll talk tonight."

Dismissed and confused, Jason left the room, bounded up the stairs, and went to his own room. This was one turn of events he had never expected.

As he lay on his bed, he replayed the scene inside his head a dozen times. His stepfather had never acted that way before. *He's never been human. What's wrong with him? Is he afraid of dying or something? What would make a mean old man like him change like that?* he wondered. *Maybe it's an answer to prayer. Maybe God has changed him.*

"I hope so," he said aloud. "Oh God, I hope so."

About twenty minutes later, he went down to Roger's office. He didn't hear anything until he was just outside the door.

". . . won't get away with this. You're a

tyrant!" That was Mr. Holmestead's voice.

The response was muffled, but he heard the words *police* and *jail*.

Mr. Holmestead swore — and those words were clear. Then his tone softened and he said, "Can't we talk — ?"

Jason turned around and went back to his room. He waited until teatime, but his stepfather walked into the dining room, sat down, and said nothing. Jason could detect no difference in his looks or attitude. He leaned close and whispered, "Uh, Dad, I wonder if we could talk." It was the first time he had called him *Dad*.

Roger shook his head. "Later. We'll talk later."

A disappointed Jason said, "Okay."

"Promise," Roger said.

Jason smiled. Roger had never used that word with him before. Something was definitely different about the old man. He even smiled when he said that single word.

As Jason sat next to his stepfather, he stared at him. Roger had a strict rule about teatime. He allowed no important conversation. Jason always thought that was stupid, but that's what the old man said. "This is the time not to think of serious issues," he said more than once.

Roger kept his conversation focused on

the weather. Holmestead commented on the impending rain. Paulette said they needed more rain. Beth Wilson commented that the state of Georgia showed a five-inch rain deficit for the year. Jason tired of listening to the small talk and found himself thinking again about the strange experience with his stepfather. He watched Roger and listened whenever he spoke, but he didn't seem any different than he had been at other times. Maybe the old man was going crazy. Maybe he had started to take drugs. He stared at the man's eyes — the first giveaway sign — but he couldn't see any unusual dilation.

Roger's gaze met his. The two stared momentarily, and Roger gave him the barest nod and a hint of a smile.

"I know it sounds weird to you, Mr. Burton, but I felt something happen inside me. Like I said, I've been praying and praying for him. When I looked at him, I loved him. *Just like that.* All my anger evaporated. That's the only way I know to say it. It was — well, like a miracle or something. He didn't look any different and he didn't say anything. But I felt as if I had changed. I wanted to get out of my chair and go over and hug him or something."

"What did you do?" Burton asked.

"Nothing. I just sat there trying to figure out what had happened to me. Maybe it was something that happened to him. I don't know."

"You felt your prayer had finally been answered, huh?"

"Yes. And you know, I did care. I still do. I wish — I wish we could have talked — even for just a few minutes. I wish I could have told him."

"Maybe he knows."

"Yeah, maybe . . ."

20

"What are you doing in here?" Julie stood in the doorway of the office.

I sat in the dark. Jason had left minutes earlier, and I sat ruminating over all the things that had transpired since I first reached Palm Island.

Julie was dressed. Different slacks, different blouse, but the same casual style. I don't know much about clothes, but she looked good in those muted colors.

"I might ask you the same question," I said.

"You might, but I asked first."

"I thought I heard someone in the hallway — or maybe I didn't. I awakened and came downstairs." I told her what happened with Jason. "Now it's your turn. What made you open the office door?"

"I don't know. I didn't have any sense of anyone being in here. Maybe I just wanted to assure myself that it was locked."

"Okay, so why did you come downstairs?" My watch showed 4:03.

"I couldn't sleep. And I got hungry again. I dressed to come downstairs and eat the rest of the Oreo cookies." Instead of going to the kitchen, she came into the office and sat down. She kept her eyes averted from Roger's body.

I moved the office sofa just enough to hide most of it. She could see only the end of the blanket. Although Simon had covered him, it was still a body. I hoped that by not seeing him, we could push him out of our consciousness.

"After Jason went back to bed," I said, "I decided to stay here in case anyone else came to pay a visit."

"Good idea," she said. She locked the door from the inside, turned off the light, and felt her way over to the sofa.

I got up and opened the blinds. A half-moon had sneaked across the horizon. Only a few scattered clouds drifted above, and the night sky was ablaze with stars.

"I keep thinking about Paulette and Jason both coming here to the office." I kept my voice low in case someone else tried to come to the office. I didn't want my voice to carry.

"I didn't even know about Jason, naturally, but I kept thinking about Paulette," Julie said. "Just suppose Roger had a file that contained the truth about everyone here on the island. Suppose he planned to confront us tonight —"

"Confront may be the wrong word. He said *announce,* didn't he?" I asked.

"Regardless of the word, wouldn't that scare some of them?"

"Did it scare you?"

Julie thought for a minute. "Not really. You know why? Roger had kept the incident a secret for years. Why would he bring it up now? I had always done whatever he asked."

"But what if some of them felt the burden had become intolerable?" I asked. "What if that led them to think he might plan to expose them?"

"That's exactly what occurred to me," Julie said. "We've already heard several confessions. Maybe the police can figure out who had the strongest motive. So far, I can't."

"Nothing quite fits into place," I said. "And what about the attempt to kill Wayne Holmestead? That just doesn't fit. We can figure out the reason for Roger's death, and we can assume that Elaine Wright saw someone or heard something."

"But where does Wayne fit in?" Julie asked.

"I don't know. That's what doesn't make sense."

We sat in silence, but I knew both our minds were working. Two people had come into the office. Both had searched for some papers. Paulette wanted her confession, and Jason wanted whatever it was his stepfather had held up. Were the searches connected with the murder? That seemed logical.

Julie said she would curl up on the large chair on the other side of the office. I wanted to act like a gentleman, so I told her to take the sofa. She lay down on the sofa, and I got on the floor and used one of the sofa cushions. She did try to dissuade me, but I assured her I could sleep on the carpeted floor.

I stretched out, loosened my shoe laces, and tried to relax. I closed my eyes, but I couldn't think of anything except the stories the people had told me. I assumed they were true — at least largely true — but even if they were, things still weren't making sense.

I wasn't aware of falling asleep, but a gentle tap at the office door startled me. I jumped up and stumbled toward the door and opened it.

"I went to your room and you weren't there," Amanda said. "I looked everywhere else downstairs and finally figured you must have come in here."

Julie sat up, rubbed her eyes, and smiled.

I looked at my watch. It was 4:38. I felt the stubble on my chin and thought about whether to opt for more sleep or a shower and shave.

"I'm so glad you're here, because I need to talk to you," she said.

"Come on in," Julie said and snapped on the light.

"I killed Roger. It was an accident, but I did it."

"Tell me what happened."

"We had an argument —"

"About what?"

"That's not important —"

"I think it is. Tell me."

"It was about Jason."

"What about him? Please, don't make me pull every word out of you."

"Jason did something bad — really bad."

"What did he do?" Julie asked.

"He forged Roger's signature on eight checks. There may have been more, but that's all I know about. He had Victoria's Secret deliver several packages of skimpy clothing. Two parcels came from some horrible place called the Super Sex Shop. Roger was appalled. Roger found out after I left him."

"When was that?" I asked.

"About three weeks ago."

"Three?" Julie said. "Are you sure?"

"It may have been only nineteen days —
but yes, it was close to three weeks. Roger
called me in Savannah and told me."

"I know about the forgery and the deliv-
ery," I said, "but are you sure it was ap-
proximately three weeks ago?"

"Yes. Why? What difference does it make?"

"It means Roger knew and didn't do
anything — not until yesterday," Julie said.
"Doesn't that seem odd?"

"Nothing Roger did would seem odd," she
said.

"How did you know about the forgery?"

"Jason came down here earlier. He told
me."

"Did he — did he tell you anything else?"

"Was he supposed to tell me something?
Come on, Amanda. I'm tired and I've
hardly slept."

"Roger was furious over what Jason had
done. He's been furious a lot of other times,
but this was — it was the worst. He swore
at me and called me names — well, terrible
names — and accused me of being a bad
mother."

"Anything else?"

"I offered to give Roger the money, and
he laughed at me. He didn't need the

money, but I was afraid —"

"Afraid of what?"

"That he would send Jason to jail. That was typical of him. Punish the guilty or punish the innocent. It didn't matter which. He was good at punishing."

"So you were angry?"

"Of course. Jason didn't need the money. He has money. I have money."

"Wait a minute," I said. "Let's get back to Roger's death. Tell us what happened."

"I was furious — the angriest I've ever been with him."

"Why?"

"He said he had — had decided to have Jason prosecuted. He would send my son to jail and he would forbid me to have any contact with him."

"That would make anyone angry," I said. I didn't believe her, but I had to play this out.

"And the gun? He kept the gun in his desk," I said. "How did you get it?"

She hesitated only a second before she said, "I lunged for the desk, pulled the drawer open, and grabbed the gun. I didn't plan to kill him. I'm not sure what I meant to do — maybe to frighten him. Yes, I only wanted to frighten him — to make him say he wouldn't send Jason to prison. When you're a mother, you —"

"When you're a mother," Julie said, "you'll do anything to protect your child, right?"

"He wanted Jason to go to prison. I couldn't allow that. Jason is a good son. He's never been in trouble before. He was — well, he had been angry and had acted stupidly. Roger didn't remember his birthday for two years in a row, and I think he just acted out of immaturity and anger and forged the checks."

"Hmm, I see."

"So tell us — what happened?" Julie asked. Something about her voice told me she didn't believe the story, either.

"We struggled. The gun went off, and Roger fell to the floor. I — I panicked and ran from the room."

"With the gun in your hand?"

"Oh yes, yes."

"What did you do with the gun?"

"I threw it over the cliff. I went out the east door — and no one saw me. I tossed it over the cliff and then raced back inside."

"When you threw away the gun, was that after you shot at Wayne Holmestead?"

"Wayne? I — I didn't shoot at him," she said. It was obvious she had forgotten to take that into account.

"I see," I said.

"And you killed Elaine, as well?" Julie asked.

"Oh no. I would never hurt Elaine. Neither would Jason. I didn't like her very much, but I felt she was badly treated by Roger."

"So there is another murderer here," Julie said to Amanda, but she looked at me. She and I were operating on the same wavelength. "You killed Roger, and then someone else killed Elaine. Why would anyone kill her?"

"I have no idea."

"Did Elaine see you leave Roger's office?" I asked.

"I'm sure she didn't. I mean, even if she had, I wouldn't have hurt her."

"I believe you," I said. "In fact, I don't think you killed anyone."

"You think Jason killed Roger," Julie said, "and you're trying to protect him. After all, isn't that what mothers do?"

"No, that's not true. I killed Roger. I've confessed. Let's leave it at that, please."

"You have watched too many TV programs," Julie said and smiled at Amanda. "Jason didn't kill him, either. Why did you think he did?"

"Jason didn't?" She dropped into a chair. "You're positive?"

"As positive as I can be until we find out who did," I said.

"Why did you think Jason killed Roger?" Julie persisted.

"It was what he said just before he went downstairs to see Roger — in the afternoon, maybe a couple of hours before tea. He said, 'I hate that man. I've tried to love him. I've tried to forgive him for making you miserable and for being such a lousy father. I'll do anything to make him suffer. Anything!'"

"So you naturally thought he killed Roger?"

She nodded.

"If Jason is the boy I think he is — and if he had killed Roger — do you think he would have allowed you to take the blame?"

"He would have stepped in and confessed," Julie said. "Isn't that the kind of kid he is?"

"I hadn't thought of that," she said. "I feel like a fool. I love my son, and he hasn't had an easy life with Roger. I only wanted to protect him. I felt I owed him that much for all he's had to go through."

"You haven't talked with Jason about this, have you?" I asked.

"No. He came upstairs before tea and said he and Roger hadn't finished their conversation. I tried to get information from him, but he said, 'Not now, Mom. I'm too confused to talk.' "

"Just that?"

"No. He turned around and said in a flat voice. 'This isn't over. Not yet. We haven't settled it yet.' "

"You're a good woman," I said. "You have a good heart."

"There is one other thing that you probably need to know. Jason did threaten to kill Roger once. I'm not sure, but I think it was maybe six months ago. We had guests here, and Wayne was one of them." Amanda said she didn't know what the argument had been about — something about school or grades. She had been weeding on the far side of the house. Just as she came in through the front door, Jason screamed at Roger, "I'll kill you! I'll do the world a big, big favor! I will kill you someday."

"So you thought he had kept that promise?"

She started to cry and barely nodded. I hugged her and said, "It must be a big relief to know that Jason didn't kill Roger."

"But if he didn't do it, and I didn't —"

"That leaves seven suspects," Julie said. "Wayne Holmestead, Jeffery Mark Dunn, Paulette White, Tonya Borders, Beth Wilson, Lenny Goss, and Reginald Ford."

"I can't believe any of them would —"

"Roger didn't kill himself," Julie said. "And we don't think Elaine's death was an accidental fall."

The three of us spoke together in hushed tones, but none of us came up with a solution.

The clock struck five. "It will be sunrise soon," I said. I debated whether to go upstairs to bed or just to have a long, hot shower. Julie and Amanda left the room. I turned the light off. As I debated what to do, I settled down into the sofa and went to sleep. I don't even remember putting my head on the cushion.

21

I don't know how long I slept, but I awakened, unsure of what startled me. The dawn had just begun. Gray light seeped in around the drapes. It was too dim to reveal the details of the furniture, but it was bright enough to deepen the shadows and distort the shape of everything, so that the room seemed like an alien place.

Julie unlocked the door and opened it only an inch or so and saw me sit up startled before she threw it fully open and snapped on the light. Simon stood next to her.

"What's going on?" I asked.

"Make coffee," he said. "We talk."

"Are you trying to sound like the old Simon?"

"I spotted Simon sneaking in the front door," she said. "I tried to talk to him, and he's reverted to his bad English again."

"Sneaking in the front door? Why?"

She shrugged, and this time I laughed.

"You do that just like Simon."

"Glad you noticed. I've practiced a lot," she said. "I think Simon was out all night. I didn't think of it then, but he was the only person not present when we found the bullet in the doorpost."

"Make the coffee. I'll be right there," I said.

My head felt rotten. I'm always grouchy until I've shaved. I'm not sure why, but my face always feels heavy, and this time it was also achy from lack of sleep. I tried to argue myself into getting off the sofa, going upstairs, and cleaning up before I confronted Simon. Instead, I closed my eyes.

The aroma of coffee filled my nostrils, and I opened my eyes. Julie smiled. "You don't snore when you sleep on your back."

Not sure where that conversation could lead, I looked at Simon, who held out a cup of coffee. I waved away the sugar and cream.

"Caught," he said. "Out all night."

"Oh, cut it out, Simon. We don't want to listen to the pidgin English anymore," I said. "I already have a headache."

"Sorry, habit." Then he laughed.

"So tell us."

"I was out all night, that's true."

"What were you doing?" Julie asked.

"That's not important for you to know," he said.

"That answer isn't good enough," I said. "As soon as the telephone is working, we'll call the police."

"The telephone is now working. I called the police. They will be here as soon as they can."

"How soon?"

"Does it matter? This is a small island, and I have the only key to the Boston Whaler." He pulled the key from his pocket. "So no one can leave before they arrive. The police know that. They will probably wait until the new shift goes on at 8:00, and then someone will come."

I looked at my watch. It was five minutes before six. "Seems like a long time."

"Does it matter?" Julie said. She held up a notebook. "I've written down everything we've learned so far, and I can tell the police. It also means that none of the other suspects can change his or her story."

"Back to you, Simon. You admit being out all night. What were you doing?"

"Praying."

"What?" Julie asked.

"I was on the beach. I prayed all night."

"*All night?* That must have been five or six hours. How long does it take to say a few

245

prayers?"

"Sometimes it takes hours."

Simon and I looked at each other, and he smiled as if to say, "Okay, I'll try to explain." He turned to her. "You see, it is more than repeating words. Prayer — the kind of prayer of which I speak — means to open my heart to God. It's not so much words I speak, as that I feel such — such a heaviness — a burden that is so heavy it makes me —"

"Oh," she said. "I see."

She obviously didn't, so I said, "He was deeply troubled. He needed to get alone and talk to God. He wanted to find inner peace. For some of us, that's how we do it: We pray. So, yes, I understand."

"Okay, I really don't understand," Julie said, "but let that go. Why aren't you soaked if you were out all night?"

"I keep a small tent in my room, and it takes ninety seconds to set up. I often put it up at night and sleep near the edge of the island. It's peaceful. But it's more than that. It's a place where I can be alone with my thoughts and with my prayers."

"Oh," Julie said. "Now I have something else I want to ask you — something I think is important."

"Of course, just ask."

"What did Roger hold over you? What is your secret?"

Shock registered in his eyes. "Why do you ask such a question?"

"Everyone else has a secret of some kind. Why should you be different?"

He smiled, and his face had a boyish look. "You're correct. In my own way, I was a prisoner here like the others." He paused to drink deeply from his coffee and poured himself a fresh cup.

"I was a lawyer — a good lawyer as a matter of fact. By age twenty-four, I had earned more than six million dollars a year by representing pharmaceutical companies in court."

"And you killed somebody or stole money or —"

He shook his head. "No. I sampled their products. That's where I got into trouble. At first, it was only an occasional upper. It's an old story, and thousands of other people have the same sad tale. A few pills on bad days. Before long, every day became a bad day. But, I reminded myself, it was only temporary until I got past this big case or until I could get my schedule down to normal. Eventually, I had to pop a couple of uppers to get going in the morning, another couple to handle the work of the

247

day — I'm sure you know how the story goes."

"So the company found out that —"

"Not exactly. I switched to meth."

"Methamphetamine?"

"Right. It's a form of speed, you know."

"I also know it's cheap to make," I said.

"That's the point. Cheap. Easy to get. I didn't have to pilfer the company's products."

"So what happened?"

"At first I thought I was free. I never had to peep over my shoulder. I forgot one thing, however —"

"Which is?"

"Drugs are drugs. And most drugs, even the most benign ones, if taken regularly and over a long period of time, become addictive. Of course I was strong and I could always kick the habit.

"Although we addicts lie to ourselves for a long time, and I did, eventually I faced a reality: I couldn't function without meth. I couldn't go to a business meeting without my own brand of insurance."

For several minutes, Simon told us his sad account of how he had wrecked his life. His wife divorced him and moved away. He had no idea where she was or where she had taken their two children. The police nabbed him one day after a high-speed chase up I-95. "I was lucky I didn't kill somebody."

He received a seven-year prison sentence.

"And you learned your lesson?" I asked.

"No, I was still the tough guy. There were ways to get drugs and there were ways to make meth. The truth was that I didn't want to kick the habit. I hated it when I was down, but when I had a hit — a good hit — there was nothing in my life that felt so good."

"You're not on drugs now," I said. "That seems obvious."

"You want to know why?" He pointed to a barely visible scar on the left side of his face. It ran from his temple to the top of his lip. "See this? This scar saved my life."

I must have looked startled, because Simon laughed. "You did that to shock me, right?" Julie asked.

"Yes, I did, but it's also true. I was a mess in prison. My entire first seven months were like a buzz of forgetfulness. As I said, there are ways to get the drugs we need." Simon told us that his cell mate was a man named Michael Kamen. "If ever there was an innocent man in prison, it was Michael." His cell mate had been accused of armed robbery. He did resemble the criminal (and the police caught the real one after Michael had served almost four years).

The two men shared common interests and both were college grads — the only ones in the prison population. They were both bright and articulate and had been successful in the corporate world. Michael had been a contract lawyer.

"Michael took no drugs, nor did he have any bad habits. He called himself a 'born-again Christian.' He cared about me and often talked to me about God. I didn't want to listen, but he talked anyway. Some nights he'd read portions of the Bible aloud or tell me what he had read in religious books. He was my friend, so I couldn't tell him to shut up." Simon laughed. "Okay, I did tell him to shut up a few times, but he never gave up.

"He was concerned about my drug habit and gently tried to talk to me about it. I tuned him out. He became stronger and more adamant. He was on my back constantly about quitting."

Michael started a Bible study group in the prison library. He successfully recruited two of Simon's drug-addicted friends. Then others came. Soon there were about fifty regular attendees, and the gangs that had run the cell block were losing their power. One hardened criminal determined to put a stop to the religious fervor. He came after Michael with a shiv.

Simon jumped into the melee, and the man with the knife attacked him. It ended when Simon broke the man's wrist. That man was moved to another prison.

"I had this cut on my cheek, but that wasn't the worst. He also struck me in the kidneys. I was rushed to a civilian hospital. For two days no one knew if I would live. Somehow Michael received permission to be there with me. He sat at my bed. Most of that time he prayed."

Simon told us that he saw the reality of love and compassion in Michael. It was Michael who made him realize how he had wasted his life.

"I was a slow learner, but Michael was patient with me. I joined his Bible study. You see, something powerful happened to me while I was in prison. I also became a born-again Christian."

"Oh yeah, like Jimmy Carter," Julie said. "Or that healing evangelist on TV."

"Okay, if you want to say it that way," Simon said with no defensiveness in his voice. "My life changed. Truly changed. It wasn't that I didn't have yearnings for meth. I did, but I also had God in my life, and I knew I would never go back."

"And did it last — that — that change?" Julie asked.

He smiled at Julie and nodded slowly before he said, "On my thirtieth birthday I was baptized. That was five years ago. I still believe. And you know, you could —"

"And Michael? What happened to him?" Julie asked, and I was sure it was more out of her discomfort than truly wanting to know the answer.

"Three months after I was baptized, Michael's sentence was overthrown, and they released him from prison."

"Ever see him again?" Julie said. "I've heard that former convicts don't like to visit."

"Michael never forgot me. He wrote regularly. Every week he visited me. He brought me books. He spoke with the chaplains about me and asked them to encourage me. Eventually I took over Michael's Bible studies."

"Oh," she said. She still wasn't comfortable, but for once Julie West didn't know what to say next.

"You've stared at my scar several times," Simon said to her.

"I didn't intend to stare —"

"It's all right." He pointed to his scar. "I could have had it removed. Roger was willing to pay for it, but I refused. It's a constant reminder that my life is different. That scar is there to tell me who I used to be and who I am now."

"Are you still in contact with Michael?" I asked.

Tears welled up in his eyes. "He died in an automobile accident just before I was released from prison."

"I am sorry —"

"I miss him every day, but I'm grateful he stayed alive long enough to share his faith and friendship with me. Sometimes I think of him as an angel from God — like Michael the archangel, you know. I know people aren't angels, but he seemed like an angel from on high to me. After I surrendered myself to God, I had a long time to think and to get my life in order. I got out of prison after four years because I didn't cause any more trouble and the parole board agreed that I had been rehabilitated. I kicked the habit in prison and began to get my life in some kind of order."

"So Roger held your past over you?" Julie asked.

"No, no, not that. I served my sentence, and I could hold up my head. No, Roger got involved because I violated my parole."

"That was stupid," she said.

"Yes."

"But you did violate it, huh?" Julie asked. "And in the process, you went back to drugs?"

"Oh no. Never." Simon stared at Julie in surprise. "I told you, I would never do that."

"Okay, how did you violate your parole?"

"That's where I was stupid."

"There are a lot of ways to be stupid," Julie said.

"I visited some of my old friends. They refer to them as 'known criminals.' They were guys I had done business with — felons — and some of them had been in prison two or three times."

"Why in the world would you go to see them if you weren't back into drugs?"

Simon turned and looked at me. "You're a preacher, you can understand this part. Something powerful had happened to me while I was incarcerated. My life had changed, and I discovered something I had never known before."

"What was that?" Julie asked.

"Peace," he said simply. "I've always been a hustler. I was one of those people who rushed, pushed, and never stopped. I graduated at the top of my college class at age twenty and had my master's degree and passed the bar before I was twenty-two." He

254

paused and played with his hands before he continued. "I guess deep inside I knew something was missing in my life, but I had no idea what it was. It took prison to slow me down enough to face myself."

"Can we skip forward to the parole violation?" Julie asked.

"Are you afraid to hear about God at work in my life?"

"Afraid? Of course not. It's only —"

"It's only that you are probably running, too, aren't you?"

"Okay, Simon, don't push it," I said. "Julie doesn't want that part of the story. I'd love to hear it, and perhaps you'll tell me more later."

"Yes, sir, I'd like that. Well, one of the things that Michael kept saying, and I think he was correct, was that it wasn't enough for me to find inner peace. My responsibility — and my privilege — was to pass it on. That's how he constantly said it. Responsibility and privilege. So two weeks after my parole, I learned where several of my old friends lived."

"So you went to their home?"

He shook his head. "I learned the name of the bar where they went regularly. Part of my parole was that I was not to go inside any drinking establishment and not to socialize with any known felons. I went to see my friends anyway. That's when the police caught me. You know, one of those random checks when they were looking for something else — I never did learn what — and they found me with four known felons. To make it worse, one of them had two kilos of hash with him. Get the picture?"

Both of us nodded.

"I pleaded with the arresting officer. I asked him for a chance. The others also told him I had come to talk to them and that I was clean."

"He wouldn't listen but took me to jail to book me. On the way I talked to him some more." Simon laughed self-consciously. "The officer stopped the car and told me to sit tight — as if I could get out of the car. With five of us handcuffed together in the backseat and the two smallest sitting on our laps, I wasn't going anyplace. Besides, the lock was on the outside of the door. The officer got out of the vehicle, walked several feet away, and used his cell phone. A couple of minutes later he got back inside. He turned around in the front seat and said, 'Presswood, this must be your lucky day.' He took me to Mr. Harden's office first, let me out, and booked the others."

"He just took you there and left you?" Julie asked.

"That's it. I met Roger Harden standing in front of his office building. I spent twenty minutes with him, and we made a deal."

"What kind of deal?"

"The kind Mr. Harden made with every one of us. Essentially, it was extortion. I didn't want to go back to jail, and he knew that. He wasn't interested in the reason I went to the bar, but he said the police officer believed in my innocence. After I gave him my word that I wouldn't run away, he put me up in a hotel and told me to come back in three days."

"Why would he do that?" Julie asked.

Simon laughed at that question. "Because he was Roger Harden. He had to show me his control. One time I started to leave the hotel to eat, and a bellman stopped me. He said I was to order from room service and not to leave my room. He was to bring me anything I needed, but I wasn't to leave."

"For three days?"

"Like being in prison again — of sorts," Simon said. "It also gave Roger time to find out everything about me. I had a phone call that said, 'Mr. Harden's car is on the way. Be in front of the hotel in fifteen minutes.' When he summoned me back — and summoned is the right word — he held up a thick file. 'This is all about you,' he said.

"The deal he offered me wasn't as bad as I had expected. He told me that if I would work for him for two full years, he would pay me well and I would never have to go back to jail. Of course, there was the downside —"

"Which was?"

"I was his private snoop. I had to constantly report on his wife, his son, and all visitors on the island. That's why I acted as if I didn't know English. That was Roger's idea. He thought it was a great trick. He was right — you'd be amazed at how freely people spoke in my presence."

"And you reported their words to Roger?"

"Every word. I didn't like it, but I had promised."

"Didn't it trouble you?" I asked.

"Very much," he said. "In all honesty, sometimes I walked away so that I didn't have to hear some things."

"How long have you worked for him?"

"Two years and two months."

"I thought you said exactly two years?" Julie said. "Why didn't you leave at the end of that time? Wouldn't he let you go?"

"I stayed for several reasons — but none of them have anything to do with his death."

"Convince us," Julie said. She had a

determined look in her eyes, and she wasn't going to let him stop now.

"He never planned to let me go. He made me sign a confession — an undated one. He had also dug up evidence of other crimes I had done — drug things. So he could easily have sent me back to prison."

"That sounds like a good reason to kill him," Julie said. "All you had to do was kill Roger Harden, get the confession back, and you were free."

"I have the confession. He gave it to me two nights ago — okay, I guess it's now three nights."

"And you're still here?"

"Yes, I was the only one to whom he gave back the implicating evidence. He told me so."

"Why you?"

"I don't know. That's the truth: I don't know."

"Let me backtrack." He turned to Julie. "This involves God again, so it may bore you. Maybe you want to make fresh coffee while I tell Mr. Burton."

"I can handle it," she said.

"A month before my two years ended, I asked him about when I could leave. He laughed at me. He said he liked me and liked the way I did things. He said I was the best servant he'd ever had and wanted to keep me a little longer."

"A little longer?" I asked. "What did that mean?"

"It meant he wasn't going to let me go. He had enough evidence on me to keep me here. Even with the statute of limitations running out, it wouldn't matter. He had enough power to keep me here the rest of my life."

"So you shot him?" Julie asked.

"I won't even answer that," Simon said. "I was angry. Hatred raged inside me, and you know what? I think he liked seeing me so angry."

"What did you do?" I asked.

"I ran out of the house — down to the water's edge — down near where we found Elaine's body. At first I just wanted to jump into the Atlantic and drown. But I had met Jesus Christ in prison. I stopped and I prayed." He looked at Julie and said, "You'll have to take my word for this, but I fell on the ground and cried out to God for help. I pleaded with God to forgive my anger and to take away my hatred."

"Did it go away?"

"Not then — not instantly. It took two days because I couldn't forgive him, and my soul was tortured. I didn't hate him, but

I wanted to be free from him. Two nights before everyone came here, I was able to forgive him."

"I can just about believe that story," Tonya Borders said. "*Just about* believe it, but not quite."

We looked up and saw her standing at the door. We had no idea how long she had been there.

She walked into the office. "Roger was not the kindest man in the world, but if he knew you had violated your parole, he would have told me. And I would have gone to the authorities."

"You seem to be an authority on Roger Harden," Julie said. "Maybe you have something to tell us."

"I loved Roger Harden. I truly loved him. If it hadn't been for Amanda — oh, well, you know how those things go."

"She's lying," Simon said.

"How dare you say I'm lying," Tonya said. "I loved him."

"Perhaps you did," Simon said, "but you also stole from him."

22

"Stole from Roger? How can you dare to say such — such a vile thing!" Tonya Borders screamed, her accent fully in place.

I didn't realize Tonya had that much of a voice range. She had always spoken in low, unemotional tones, but her voice now reached a semihysterical pitch.

She turned from Simon and faced me. "This — this convicted criminal stands before you and dares to accuse *me* of a crime. How dare he!" She pulled off her glasses and wiped the perspiration from her face. "I told you: I loved Roger."

"Love I don't know about," Simon said. "But I know you stole from him."

"This is preposterous," she said. "Burton. Julie. Are you going to listen to this — this convicted felon?"

"I know what Roger told me."

"Oh, now that he is dead, you become familiar and call him by his first name?

What kind of person are you?"

"He asked me to call him Roger, and I have done that for the past three days. Something else — I became his friend." He looked at me and added, "That's why I didn't leave. He told me I could go. He offered to do what he could to help me get my license restored or do whatever I wanted so I could obtain a good job. He also promised to help me find my wife — my former wife — and see if there was a chance for reconciliation."

"Why didn't you go?" Tonya asked.

"He needed me," Simon said simply. "He needed me."

"How preposterous," Tonya said. "That was his problem: Roger never needed anybody."

"Let's get this back on topic," Simon said. "I accused Tonya of stealing from Roger."

"And I said —"

"Yes, I know what you *said*," Simon interrupted, "but —"

"Are you going to listen to that — that convict? I would not do such a thing as —"

"Roger said that you had falsified records and that he could prove you had cheated him out of slightly over six million dollars."

"I did not steal from Roger."

"I believe she is telling the truth." Wayne

Holmestead stood in the doorway. I have no idea how long he had been listening to the discussion. He came inside and took Tonya's hand. "You don't have to listen to such — such ridiculous charges."

"I know what I know," Simon said. "And besides —"

"Besides nothing! I was Roger's partner and best friend for more than twenty years. I was his business adviser. If Tonya had cheated or stolen anything, I would have been the first to know."

"Unless you were part of it," Simon said.

"How dare you!" Wayne raised his fist — something that seemed totally out of character.

"I know what Roger told me! Even better, I can prove it!" Simon said.

"Oh sure, the convict now becomes the police sleuth," Wayne said. "Who would listen to you?"

"You don't have to *listen* to me," Simon said softly. "All you have to do is read." He stepped so close to Wayne that he was less than six inches from his face. "You can read, can't you?"

Wayne stepped back and turned to me. "Will you get this — this person — out of here?"

"Why don't we all calm down and let Simon talk?" I said. "You'll have an opportunity to refute whatever he says."

"I'll even bring in chairs for everyone." Before anyone could protest, Simon rushed out of the room and came back with two chairs from the dining room.

"Now if Wayne and Tonya will be quiet, I'll tell you what I know."

Tonya started to object, but Wayne held up a hand. "Let him talk."

"Roger wrote something — I don't know what it said — I mean specifically. He planned to read it to us last night. I do know this much. It concerned all of us. Roger had held all of us captive to his capricious will for years. He had everything documented. He put the documentation inside a folder along with the paper he planned to read."

"Oh sure," Wayne said. "And I suppose now you're going to whip out the document and point out who killed Roger and poor Elaine and also tried to kill me."

"Why don't you give your mouth a rest?" Simon said.

Julie laughed, but the rest of us stared in shock. Such a statement from Simon seemed out of character. But then, Simon had portrayed a character whom Roger had created, and none of us had known who he truly was.

"I have the document. I haven't read it, but it's in my possession." Simon paused and let the words sink in.

"You have the documents?" Tonya repeated numbly. "All of them?"

"Everything," Simon said.

Tonya and Wayne stared at each other. I tried to read their faces, but I couldn't understand what was going on.

"Yesterday morning Roger called me into his office, and we talked for perhaps forty minutes, maybe a little longer. What we talked about isn't significant except for what he said just before I left the room."

"I suppose he told you someone would try to kill him," Tonya said, and the snicker was on her face as well as in her voice.

Simon shook his head. "He certainly had no idea that anyone would murder him. In fact, he told me about his plans."

"Plans? What plans? He certainly never discussed anything with me," Wayne said. He started in on his being Roger's friend and confidant.

Simon waited until Wayne stopped speaking and continued as if he had not been interrupted.

"Roger called me into his office. And just to make the relationship clear, he didn't order me. He saw me walking from the kitchen toward the front door. 'If you have a few minutes, Simon, could you come in here?' Those were his words. Not a command as you said —"

"Summons," Julie said. "That was the word they used. A summons."

"Whatever the word," Simon said, "Roger asked me to sit down. He told me about the dinner party and that everyone would stay overnight. He said, 'I have something here.' He held up a manila folder filled with papers. It was about two inches thick, and a rubber band held the folder tight. He slipped the folder into a large envelope and laid it on his desk."

"So where is this — this alleged envelope?" asked Tonya. "I don't see it."

"I stole it," Simon said.

"You did what?" Wayne asked.

"Whoever killed Roger wanted the envelope. I figured that out immediately, so I took it and hid it." He turned to me and said, "You see, the murderer didn't know — at least not then — that the important material was in an envelope."

"This is most confusing — and perhaps a little too melodramatic for my tastes," said Tonya.

Simon sank into a chair and turned his attention to Wayne. "You claimed to be his friend. You were the worst among us here. Roger trusted you. He thought of you as a brother — a brother he never had. He felt more betrayed by you — and by Tonya — than he did the others."

"What others?" Paulette White stood in the doorway with Jeffery Dunn and Beth Wilson next to her.

"It looks as if everyone is here except Amanda, Jason, Lenny, and Reginald," Julie said. "Why don't we all go into the drawing room and get comfortable? Simon has some interesting things to tell all of us."

"This is totally prepos—"

"Just stuff it," Simon said to Wayne. "Let me have my say, and then you can object or squirm." He laughed. "I think you'll tend to squirm."

"Let's all calm down and go into the drawing room," I said.

No one objected. Amanda and Jason were in the kitchen, and they must have heard us, because they came through with coffee and tea. Julie ran upstairs to get Reginald and Lenny.

Simon called me aside and hurriedly gave me information that shocked me. He also told me what he planned to do when we were all gathered. "Are you sure you can pull this off?" I asked. He gave me the old

Simon shrug, put his arm around my shoulder, and led me into the drawing room.

"I'm going to cook omelets," Amanda said. "Is that all right? It's about the only thing I can cook besides scrambled eggs."

"We don't need any food now," I said. "We'll stay here in the drawing room. The coffee and tea are fine. Simon wants to talk to all of us."

"Why don't we wait for the other two?" Tonya said with a smirk. "We don't want anyone to miss out on this — this fabulous tale we're about to hear."

In less than five minutes all of us were gathered in the drawing room. Several more minutes lapsed before everyone had poured themselves something to drink. I opted for water and sipped from my glass.

"Simon started to tell me several things," I said, "and most of your names came up in the middle of it. I'd like Simon to start from the beginning and tell us everything."

Tonya sighed. "Must we go through — ?"

"I would like to hear," Amanda said and stared at Tonya. "This is my house, and you're my guest."

"Wow, Mom!" Jason clapped his hands. "I wish you'd done more of that in the past."

"Be quiet, Jason," she said softly. "Let's listen."

"You're cool! Mom, you rock!"

Simon waited until everyone had given him his or her attention. I smiled at that. It was as if he were in a courtroom and we were the jury.

"Roger and I became friends quite recently," he said. "He opened up to me and talked to me."

"I can hardly believe he would discuss anything with you," Jeffery said.

Simon held up a hand. "Then indulge me. After you've heard everything, you can decide whether I'm telling the truth." He smiled and added, "Please."

As if he were making his closing arguments in a criminal trial, Simon paced the room and stared at us one at a time. "Each of us is guilty of a crime. Each of us has something to hide — something illegal we have done — and something we want to keep hidden. It is also something that Roger knew and held over us."

Without giving anyone a chance to interrupt him, he told us that Roger had discovered all of our crimes, even though he had no idea how Roger had learned everything. "He loved having you under his control. He didn't want anything except control." He walked up to each person and pointed a finger at each one.

As he walked, I found it interesting that as soon as he approached a person, stopped, and stared into that person's face, none of them could return the stare.

Not even me.

Simon's talk forced me to think about things I didn't want to contemplate. Yes, Roger had control over me, as well. I had not mentioned that to anyone, not even Julie when she confessed so openly.

Julie stared at me. Her lips formed the words, "You, too?"

I nodded and looked away. I was too ashamed to look at her again. From then on, I avoided meeting her glaring eyes.

"Everyone here is guilty — and I am guilty, as well."

"I can't stand any more of this grandstanding," Wayne said and pulled down his vest. "This is like one of those cheap crime dramas on TV where you gather everyone together and call out the murderer —"

"Of course you can't stand anymore," Simon said quietly and pointed his finger at Wayne. "I know about you. You stole from Roger. You had a scheme going, and you systematically pilfered over the years. Notice I used the word *pilfer.* He knew you had accumulated nearly a million."

"That is a lie — a terrible —"

Simon leaned forward and placed his arms on Wayne's shoulders. "He had less respect for you than anyone in this room. You know why? He said you were a cowardly crook. It took you twenty years — twenty years — to steal a million. He said you took such small amounts and you could have taken more. He said you were a total coward."

"That's not true. Not true." His voice lacked conviction, and he dropped his head.

"You were here in the afternoon. I saw Jason leave. I heard you with him. I know he showed you the letter and maybe the folder — whatever he wrote. He did, didn't he?"

"No, he showed me nothing. We talked — we talked about a riverfront project at Brunswick. He wanted to dump the project after I had invested months of time and effort and —"

"Stop lying!" Simon said. "Stop talking. Listen!" When he had control of the group again, Simon said, "I have the documents — although I have not read anything."

"So now you're going to tell us that Roger entrusted you with them? You, a convicted criminal," Tonya said.

"He didn't give them to me, remember. I stole them." Simon explained that when we rushed into the office, he saw the envelope on the desk. While everyone stared at

Roger's body, he pulled the envelope off the desk and stuck it in the back of his pants. "It's like this. Wayne knew about the letter, and he knew about the documentation, but he didn't know where it was. Possibly some of the others knew. I thought the police would get here last night, so I was going to hold it and give it to them."

"What does it contain?" I asked.

"I can only surmise," Simon said. "Roger had shown me the letter and the documentation. I don't think Wayne saw it. If so, he would have grabbed it, right? No one would have had to search the office again."

"If I had killed Roger," Wayne said, "which I didn't."

Simon walked around the room and finally said, "Whoever killed Roger Harden wanted the evidence. And I still have it."

"If you have the envelope," I said, "why don't you show it?"

"It's in my room," he said. "I can go and get it, but I'm not sure it's something to show everyone. If it's what Mr. Harden said it was, it contains information about everyone in this room."

As Simon and I had planned, I said, "Go and get it. I'll see that no one leaves the room while you're gone."

I expected Wayne or one of the women to

273

grumble about the procedure, but no one did. I had no idea about the contents, but I knew I didn't want everyone in the room to know about my past. There was no ethical way I could display the contents and not show my secrets if Roger had included mine.

As soon as Simon came back into the drawing room, Wayne tried to rip it from his hands. "As his best friend and adviser, I should look at it first."

Simon pushed him away. "No." He thrust a thumb into Wayne's chest. "I think you killed him. I'll continue to believe that until I find evidence to the contrary. So you won't be the person to open the envelope."

"How dare you —"

"You killed Roger to prevent his reading his announcement to all of you, didn't you?" I said, hardly aware of the words until they tumbled out of my mouth.

23

"No no —" Wayne said. "It's true I wanted to get rid of the letter. It wasn't just about me. Remember, Simon said that. I didn't kill Roger." He dropped his head. "I wanted to destroy the letter."

"You knew about this material," Simon said. "I have the documentation you wanted."

"Wait a minute," I said. I turned to Paulette. "You knew about the documentation, didn't you?"

"How would I know?" she asked.

"What were you searching for in Roger's desk?" Julie asked. "That had to be it. You knew about the letter or whatever it was Roger wanted to announce. You wanted to find the letter and the proof so you could destroy it all."

"That is a pathetic lie," she said. "But quite imaginative."

"We'll get back to Paulette in a moment,"

Simon said. "But first, I want to accuse Wayne Holmestead — and I don't have to read the contents of this envelope."

"How dare you!"

"The reason I have said nothing until now is that he had to have had an accomplice. She searched for this." Simon held the envelope so that everyone could see it. "The only way she could have known about the documentation was by being in cahoots with the killer."

"Maybe she killed him herself," I suggested.

Simon shook his head. "No, I know who killed Roger."

"You think I did it?" Wayne Holmestead said.

"I know you did," Simon said. He turned to the rest of us. "Remember the little incident with the gun last night. Wayne said someone had shot at him and missed."

"Everyone knows that," Beth said.

"So someone else had to have had the gun, right?"

"If we assume it was the same gun."

"Oh it was." Simon reached inside his pocket and pulled up a plastic bag. Inside was a gun. "It's a .32 caliber Beretta, and it holds seven shots. I'm sure the police will discover that it has been fired twice. It's not a bad weapon if the person knows how to use it. This Beretta has a three-and-five-eighths-inch barrel that —"

"We don't need a lecture about guns," Amanda said. "Especially — especially *that* one — if it's — if it's the — the weapon."

"Oh, it is the weapon all right," Simon said. "Would you like to know how I found it?"

"Sure — right inside Roger's desk," Paulette said. "That ought to be proof enough —"

"Then it would have to have my fingerprints on it, right?" Simon smiled. "The police will be here soon. You'll notice it's inside a plastic bag. There will be fingerprints on the gun, and they won't be mine."

"What are you trying to say?" Amanda asked.

"They will have Wayne's prints on it. I'm sure they'll also have Paulette's on it."

A visibly shaken Wayne said. "I — I don't — I don't —"

"Save your breath," Simon said. "Wayne, you killed Roger Harden, and Paulette was your accomplice — or the other way around."

Wayne shook his head violently. "No! I wouldn't — I wouldn't —"

"Oh yes, you did."

"By what brilliant process of logical deduction did you arrive at such a conclusion?" Paulette asked. She folded her arms across her chest. Her look defied Simon to prove his allegations.

"Two things," I said before Simon could reply. "First, you had to know about the document or you wouldn't have searched the office —"

"You can't prove that's what I wanted."

"No, that's true, and that's only circumstantial," I said. "Simon and I have discussed this. After I told him about the gunshot, both of us figured out something obvious — there had to be an accomplice."

"So why me?"

"We made an assumption. Because you were the person we discovered going through Roger's desk. We assumed —"

"And fingerprints," Simon said. "Unless you wiped your prints off the gun, I'm sure they'll find at least one or two."

"That's right," I said. "And how else would your fingerprints get on the gun? Someone other than Wayne had to have fired the gun in the hallway, which was obviously a ruse to throw suspicion off Wayne. The accomplice fired from somewhere down the hallway. Wayne couldn't have fired the single shot and run down to his room.

He's too large a man to run silently. Besides, even if he could have, he had no way to know that others wouldn't run from their rooms in time to see him. So, like Simon says, unless you wiped the gun clean, your fingerprints will also be on the Beretta."

"I agree with all that," Julie said, "but, Simon, how did you get the gun?"

"Yes, how did you?" Paulette said. "Maybe you're the one who fired. None of us saw you upstairs after the shot."

Simon stared at me, and I said, "Tell them."

"Last night I was broken up. I had just begun to know Roger. I can't say I knew him well, but we had an excellent beginning of —"

"We don't have to hear the entire commentary," Jeffery said. "Just tell us what happened."

"I went out to the beach to pray."

"In the rain?" asked Paulette. "I hardly believe that."

Simon explained again about the small tent. "I like to go there so I can be alone with my thoughts and with my prayers."

"Prayers?" asked Paulette. "Now you're going to tell us that you're some kind of saint who —"

"I was a lawyer and a drug addict," Simon

279

said quite simply, "and then I became a convicted criminal. After my release from prison, I went to work for Roger. Like many of you did when he learned of your crimes."

"Are you trying to call us criminals?" Paulette asked.

"I am not *trying*," he smiled at her. "The difference between me and the rest of you is that I have paid for my crimes."

"How dare you!" Wayne said. He grabbed for the plastic bag.

I took the bag from Simon. "He dares, Wayne, because it's the truth," I said. "Now let him finish."

"You see, I became a serious Christian during my time in prison. My life and my values changed and —"

"Oh dear, here comes the awful story of his rehabilitation in prison and a lengthy sermon," Paulette said. "Can we skip that, please?"

"Just listen to him," Julie said. "He might make sense."

"This is so totally okay," Jason said.

Paulette dropped her gaze.

Simon told us that he went down to the beach. He referred to the oak tree that Mrs. Wright often climbed. "I made space on the ground next to the tree. It gave me a wonderful view of the mainland — when the weather permitted." He told us the rain ended shortly after midnight. He did not hear any shots, although he did see the lights go on at one point. He considered going up to the house but decided instead to remain and pray.

"My heart was heavy. I had lost someone — Roger — who had become important to me. I agonized in prayer for God to intervene and to help us solve this heinous crime." He told us that God had given him a deep love for his former extortioner.

"Sometime after midnight — I didn't notice the time — but the rain had stopped. I was still inside my tent, kneeling in the dark. I heard footsteps on the gravel path. I wondered if someone wanted me to do something. Roger used to call me at any hour of the day or night when I was inside the house. By my being outside, he would have to come down to look for me.

"There was just enough of a moon peeking through the clouds for me to see who it was. Wayne Holmestead walked right past me — he stopped maybe five feet away. He couldn't have seen me. Then my conscience bothered me and I wondered if he needed anything. I started to speak, but he took something from his pocket and threw it over the cliff, turned around, and walked rapidly toward the house.

"That made me curious, of course," Simon said. He had a small flashlight in his tent and walked to the cliff. "I could see nothing — my flashlight isn't very powerful." He walked down the ladder and looked around. He spotted the gun. "The nose of the gun had stuck in the sand, and the handle was straight up. It was barely on the rocks. When the tide changed again and started to come in, the gun would have been washed away." He pulled off his shirt and used it to grab the gun, which he carried up to the kitchen and put into a plastic bag.

"Why didn't you come in then?" I asked.

"I wanted to pray for Wayne."

"For me? Why would you pray for me?"

"I knew you must be deeply troubled. I knew you had reacted as you did because of something Roger held over you. I prayed for God to be merciful to you and to forgive you."

"Simon came into the house a little earlier," I said, "and he told me what happened on the beach."

"So this is all settled and we can go back to bed," Lenny said. "Good show, Simon!"

"There is something else," Julie said. "The envelope. The documents Roger had."

"Oh yeah," Lenny said. "I had forgotten."

"Or maybe you wanted to forget," Beth said.

"If this were a made-for-television movie," Lenny said, "Wayne would try to make a run for it right now."

"Don't be stupid," Wayne said.

"Well, did you murder him?" Julie said.

"No, I didn't murder him." His lips quivered, and he said, "but I did kill him."

"Shut up!" Paulette said.

"Leave him alone," I said to Paulette. "Let him tell us his story."

"I did kill him, but — but it was an accident. We fought over the gun, and it went off."

"Really?" Julie asked. "How did the gun come into the argument? I thought it was kept in a desk drawer."

"Roger pulled it out. He threatened me. He said he'd shoot me if I didn't leave."

"I think you're lying," I said. "But that will be for the police and the courts to decide."

"Why did you kill Elaine?" Julie asked.

"I didn't kill her. Yes, I did kill Roger. But I don't know anything about her death."

"What's the difference?" Julie asked. "One murder or two? And it will at least be one murder and an attempt to cover it up."

"All right, I did kill him. But, it truly was

283

an accident, even if you don't believe me. I was the one who pulled out the gun. He held the letter in his hand. He started to read it. I lunged for the paper — it was actually four pages — and he pulled back, and we fought."

"Maybe," I said, "but there doesn't seem to be any sign of a struggle. Nothing was messed up. Nothing was out of place. Everyone can testify to that. Right?"

"Did you get the paper you wanted so badly?" I asked.

"No, I panicked and ran."

"You're lying," Julie and I both said at the same time.

"Sure he is," Jason said. "Nothing was messed up in the office. I saw that. I mean, it looked as orderly as Dad's desk ever did."

"The more you lie, the more difficult it will become for you," I said. "Why don't you confess before the Brunswick police arrest you?"

He sat quietly and said nothing. "Just leave me alone for a few minutes," Wayne said. "Please. I — I want to think."

I walked into the dining room and poured myself a cup of coffee.

The morning sun slanted through the slats of the blinds, striping the table with shadows and golden light. I peeked through the blinds. The sun was a warm, bright yellow ball that seemed to chase every cloud off the horizon.

Several others followed me into the dining room. I poured a cup of coffee for Wayne. Although I had no idea how he took it, I added sugar and cream. When I walked back into the drawing room, I handed him the cup on a saucer.

He nodded his thanks but didn't look at the cup. Automatically he raised it to his lips and took a long swallow. He took two more, drained the cup, and handed it back to me. Simon stood behind me to take the dirty cup back to the dining room.

He nudged me, and I followed him out.

"I'll put Wayne's cup into a plastic bag," Simon said, "It will make it easier for them to compare fingerprints."

"You're an amazing man," I said and struck him lightly on the shoulder.

"Yes, I know."

A minute later we both walked back into the drawing room.

Wayne stared at Simon and then at me. He dropped his head. "I killed Roger, but I didn't kill Elaine. That was Paulette's doing."

"What? How dare you implicate me?" Paulette said. "You think that if you throw some of this onto me that it will make it easier for you? How dare you —"

I faced Paulette, put my hands on her shoulders, and gently pushed her back into her chair. "You'll have a chance to speak," I said softly.

Holmestead turned away from her and directed his attention to me as if we were alone in the room. "Paulette and I were both in the office. She came in two or three minutes after Jason left. Elaine saw her — saw both of us."

Paulette said, "That's a lie —"

"Shut up," Simon said. "I am strong enough to tie you up and tape your mouth if I need to do so."

As ludicrous as that sounded, Paulette shut her mouth, but the anger was apparent on her face.

"Elaine also saw us come out of the office," Wayne said.

"Why didn't she tell us?" I asked. "She could have saved herself, as well."

"Money," Wayne said.

"You mean blackmail?" Julie asked.

He nodded. "She didn't know I had shot Roger — not then — but she had seen us. We were the last ones out of the office. After the discovery of the body, while we were all standing around, Mrs. Wright pulled Paulette aside. She whispered that she had seen us coming out of the office."

"That's not —" Paulette said, but she stopped when Simon came toward her.

"She told Paulette that she had heard the shot and saw us leave the office."

"And — ?" I asked.

"Paulette asked her to be quiet and said that we'd talk to her later. She told me that Mrs. Wright had also said, 'Be sure to bring your checkbook.' "

"That isn't true," Paulette said. "I have no idea why you want to implicate me, Wayne. You're guilty. You've said so. Don't try to smear me with —"

"But it was your idea to kill Mrs. Wright," he said. "That's why."

"Suppose you finish telling us, Wayne," I said.

"I don't know the details." Wayne said that Paulette told him about Mrs. Wright's comments. Wayne wanted to pay her off, but Paulette said that was never the way to work with blackmailers. Roger had never let them go and planned to expose them. "She said, 'Leave Mrs. Wright to me. You took care of Roger. I'll take care of her.' That's all I know."

"So the two women met on the cliff, and she pushed Mrs. Wright off."

"Yes."

"That's a lie!" Paulette said. "The note part is right, and I did go to the cliff, but he came, too. You know there is a large magnolia tree near the oak where Mrs. Wright used to go? He stood behind it."

"But that's a dozen feet or more from the cliff," I said.

"That's right," she said. "Mrs. Wright said she would keep quiet if we paid her two hundred thousand dollars. Wayne and I had decided that I would get her to the precipice, and he'd come up behind her and hit her and push her over the cliff. He had a hammer in his hand. She never heard him coming."

"I didn't — I didn't —" his voice broke.

"Oh, shut up," Julie said. "Don't go sniveling now."

"Now I can tell you more," Simon said. "Roger knew that Wayne and Paulette had stolen from him. What they did not know is that he wasn't going to expose them."

24

"Not expose them?" I asked. "Wasn't that the point of the invited guests and dinner meeting with all of us?"

"No, that wasn't the point," Simon said. He smiled at us. "Roger was going to forgive all of you."

"Forgive us?" Julie echoed.

"And then he was going to ask you to forgive him."

"Roger was going to ask us to forgive him? Impossible." Tonya shook her head and laughed. "Roger never made mistakes. He only capitalized on other people's failures."

"Hard to believe, but it's also true."

"How do you know that?" Jeffery asked.

"He told me." He held up the envelope. "I did not see what was inside, and I haven't looked. I didn't think it was ethical to do that." He smiled. "Yes, I have ethics. I didn't before I became a Christian, but —"

"Do spare us the sermon," Paulette said.

"Just speak up, and then shut up."

"I'll do that," Simon said and handed me the envelope. I took the envelope and opened it. There was a three-page letter and a manila folder held together by a rubber band. I pulled out the letter and skimmed it.

"And, of course," Beth said to Simon, "you took out the incriminating evidence about you."

"Beth. Everyone. Let's stop. I'll read the letter or announcement or whatever it is. As you'll see, this is what Roger planned to read to us last night." Burton began to read.

I've decided to put this in writing because I want to say everything correctly. I don't want to get sidetracked with questions or comments — I'll respond to them when I've finished.

First, I have been a businessman — a successful businessman — since I was in my early twenties. As a human being, I was a failure. I failed as a husband and certainly failed as a father to Jason. I have been underhanded and manipulative and interested only in myself.

"I don't think we need to sit here and listen to Roger's sad, dull, and soulful experience," Beth said. "I've heard better things at AA meetings." She smiled and said, "Yes, I am a member of AA and also Narcotics Anonymous. That's another little story that our dear, departed Roger knew."

"Read it anyway," Amanda said. "I want to hear it. I — I need to hear it."

I read the first page, and it was mostly what I'd call confessional information. He didn't mention anyone individually but said that he had gained power by finding human weaknesses and wrongdoings and exploiting them.

He also wrote that those invited here were not the only people of whom he had taken advantage.

There are others — hundreds of others. I've written to many of them, and I'm in the process of contacting others. I had a luncheon last week with nine other people and went through what I plan to do here tonight.

I wanted to see each of you in person. In many ways, you are the people who should have been closest to me for various reasons. I didn't allow any of you to get close, to know me well, or to care for me. I pushed you aside. I know that caused you to detest me. You liked what I could do for you, but you didn't like the price you had to pay.

I've already told you about the change in my life. I want to tell you what brought it about. Three months ago my life shattered. One person I had blackmailed took his own life. He sent me a letter that arrived after his death. He said he couldn't take it any longer.

In the letter, he reiterated all the demeaning things I had done to him and the demands I had made of him. He was totally correct. I had thought only of power. It had never occurred to me how deeply oppressed people felt. That was the first time in my life I saw myself as evil.

I stopped reading momentarily. Except for a few of us who knew what had happened to Roger, the rest were in shock at this unexpected turn of events. I had expected Lenny to interrupt with smart comments, but he sat there, his mouth open, and stared.

"I'm so — so happy to know Roger changed," Amanda said. "For years I tried to talk to him about God, but he refused to listen. However, I never stopped praying — not even after I left him." Tears burst from her, and she wept with a lack of self-consciousness and control. Instead of decreasing, her crying grew louder.

For several minutes, her sorrow and pain seemed to fill the room. Her wailing gave the rest of us an opportunity to realize the impact of Roger's letter.

"I wish we had known," Lenny said. "I can't tell you the number of times I've wished he'd get run down by a car or killed by a mugger."

"It hardly seems like the same Roger Harden I have known for all these years," Jeffery said. "I did not know he was capable of emotion of any kind."

I should have stopped Jeffery then, but he began a monotoned lecture about how we never know other people and how little we understand their feelings.

"Yes, that's true," Julie interrupted him. "But let's get back to Roger's letter."

I smiled my thanks to her. The others must have felt the same way, because I heard affirmations and saw nodding heads.

Until then, I had not thought I'd harmed anyone. I rationalized that I always gave them more than I took. I opened doors, gave them investment opportunities, or hired them. I thought it seemed like a good bargain from their point of view.

I say "rationalized" because that's what

it was. I didn't care about what others felt. I wanted to have control over them. It was a compulsion that would not let go. It sounds easy enough for me to say it, but I never wanted to do damage to anyone — certainly not enough so that someone would feel the only way to be free of me was to take his own life.

That man's death rocked me emotionally. Nothing had ever shaken me so badly. Although he did not say it, I knew his death was on my hands. I had murdered that poor, foolish man.

I couldn't get away from the shame — the overwhelming shame and guilt. I felt as if I were the most miserable and despised person in the world. I didn't like anything about myself. How could I? I had destroyed many lives.

I realized the reason several of my trusted employees — or those I should have trusted — had stolen from me. That was their way to avenge themselves. My first inclination had been to ruin their lives, but I knew I couldn't live with myself if I caused another person's death.

I decided to get help. I met with a therapist, and he suggested I also talk with a minister. He said he felt my problems were also spiritual in nature.

Roger's letter told us that he had consulted a pastor and met with him regularly. He read several books, and every day he read portions of the Bible. At times he hated what he read in the Bible, but he kept coming back. He said that I had greatly influenced him because of what I had done for Jason. Most of all, Simon was the one who had touched him. He said that both of us had badly flawed pasts and had overcome them. We were an inspiration to him.

Yes, I became a believer. But I wanted to do more than believe. Because I believed, I wanted my life to change. I had heard of people who had great emotional experiences. That was not mine. I had discovered peace — a deep, deep inner peace. I knew God had forgiven me. The minister urged me to contact everyone I had wronged and ask their forgiveness.

That is why I called you here. I have saved every paper or document I have used against you. I wanted you to be here tonight so that I can give them to you and you may destroy them yourselves.

I have chosen to forgive you.

Two of you are here because you have been systematically stealing from me. I will erase that. I can no longer allow you to work for me, but I will do nothing to prosecute you or prevent your getting a new position. For the others, I will do whatever I can to help you in any way I can.

I have only one thing to ask of you: I ask you to forgive me. I have been a tyrant and I have been evil. I know God has erased my sins, and I plead with you to forgive me.

"You knew?" Amanda asked Simon. "You knew he had become a believer and you didn't tell me?"

Simon nodded. "Blame me that he said nothing. I may have been wrong — and if so, I apologize. I suggested that he tell no one, and he agreed with me."

"Why? Why wouldn't you want everyone to know?"

"In time he needed to tell everyone, but first I wanted to see Roger change. I have known many who had what we called jailhouse conversions. They had powerful experiences, but once they received parole or their parole was refused, they lost their Christianity."

"That makes sense," Jason said. "I *saw* the difference the day he died. It wasn't just the things he said to me, but I knew — I knew something had changed." He hugged his mother. "I hope that will give you peace to know that he is in God's presence right now."

"You see, Amanda, Roger wanted to reconcile with you," Simon said. "He wanted to tell you — in the presence of these people." His hand swept to indicate everyone in the room. "He wanted you to know that you were the most important person in his life. He felt he had hurt you the most by his demanding ways. He wanted you to forgive him."

"To forgive him?" Amanda broke out in fresh tears. "I prayed, but I never believed — not really — that he would change."

"He changed. He also wanted you to help him grow. Once he became a believer, he was able to look back at the way you lived. He told me that you were far, far kinder to him than he deserved."

"She was," Jason said. "That's part of the reason I hated him. Mom let him yell at her. Sometimes he acted as if she was an idiot or a first grader."

Simon smiled, and his eyes moistened. "In some ways, he was like a boy himself — after his change. He had found something wonderful, better than anything he had experienced before, and he wanted to be the one to share the news. I respected that right."

"He was going to tell us at dinner," Jason said. "I knew — sort of — that something had happened. I'm a believer, too. That's part of what helped me forgive Dad."

"This is quite extraordinary, isn't it?" Reginald said. "Our two murderers committed unnecessary acts of violence. Of course, murder is always unnecessary, but Roger was going to forgive them. If they had only waited." He shook his head in wonderment.

"Why didn't he tell me?" Wayne wailed. "If he'd just hinted —"

"Did you give him a chance?" I asked.

"No, perhaps not." He hung his head. "Roger said, 'I know what you've done. I know the money you've stolen from me. That's why I've called you here to the island.' He smiled at me and said, 'I have a major announcement to make.' It didn't occur to me that he would forgive me. Certainly not Roger Harden. I expected him to step on me as if I were a mere bug. So I screamed at him that he couldn't do that. I knew where he kept the gun. I grabbed it, and I shot him." He stared at the floor. "You know all the rest."

The ringing of the telephone interrupted

the conversation. Jason ran to Roger's office and picked up the phone. He returned to the room. "The police are on their way. They'll be here in about ten minutes."

I read the final portion of the letter, which was a beautiful prayer for all of us to follow God in our lives. I replaced the letter in the envelope.

"Aren't you going to show us the documentation?" Reginald said. "If Roger was going to forgive us, then why — ?"

"Isn't that a matter for the police?" I said.

"But what if they read it? Our lives will be ruined, too," said Lenny.

I gave him my best Simon-imitation shrug.

25

This is Julie picking up again. I didn't know what Simon and Burton planned, but it worked. I do know what happened after the police came.

Everything considered, that final event was a great climax to the evening and morning. It took us about half an hour to explain everything to the two police officers. Simon would talk, and I'd interrupt with information he'd forgotten, and then Burton would remind us of something else.

The one in charge was a woman. The other, who was new to the force, stood and observed, but he never said a single word. By the time we finished, the woman officer said, "I hope you can remember everything you've told me."

That's the reason both of us are writing. It's not to show each other. I'd blush if Burton knew how I felt about him — especially at our first meeting to travel to Palm Island together. No, I'm writing down everything so I can remember if it comes to trial. Wayne Holmestead is such a wimp, and he can't seem to confess enough. Paulette has denied she did anything wrong. She finally said Wayne had coerced her. She claimed Wayne killed Elaine. I'm not sure it makes much difference who did what. Eventually, she did admit that they were both guilty.

Oh yes, they found Paulette's fingerprints on the gun, and Wayne's — oh, but that came out nearly two weeks later.

We had one important moment of excitement, and I have to write it so I remember every detail. After the police officer heard the story, and after both Wayne Holmestead and Paulette White admitted to her and to the rest of us that they had killed Roger, she asked for the envelope.

"I have a question," Burton said. "We are all witnesses that Wayne and Paulette confessed to two murders. Is that correct?"

Everyone agreed.

"There was no coercion. No force used. Right?" Burton said and grinned.

Simon caught on, and he grinned. "Great idea! Yes!"

I stared at both of them, and then I caught on. I was a little slow on that one. I supposed I grinned in imitation of the two men.

"So you don't need this envelope." Burton held it up for the police officer to see.

"Not to convict, but it is evidence, you know."

"And it could be used to harm all of us, right?" I said. I winked at my two conspirators.

"If you've committed crimes, then of course it would be evidence and I would have to use any information against you."

"Even if we were all blackmailed? Even if we've all more than paid for our crimes?"

"That is not for me to decide," she said. "You hand me evidence. My job is to take it to my superiors. I bring in the evidence, and they make the decisions."

"Think about the material in the envelope," I said. I didn't look at her, but at the others in the room.

"We all know one part of the contents — our own, uh, failures — but I'm sure there was more. Is that correct?"

Everyone agreed.

"That's correct," Simon said. "If the police officer takes the envelope and the contents are revealed, who will it harm?"

"I have a wife and two teenage girls," Reginald said. "I would hate for them to know."

"It would kill my mother," Jeffery said.

"She has always been proud of me." He looked around. "She's in a nursing facility, you see."

"Please — please don't give it to her," Amanda said. "There are some things in there about me, but that's not my concern. Look at all the lives this can ruin. It will be exactly the opposite of what Roger wanted."

"Exactly what I was thinking," Burton said. He turned to the police officer. "I am going to burn this. You may accuse me of destroying evidence, but I'm going to burn it anyway."

He walked across the room, and the officer made no attempt to stop him. If she had, I think she knew the rest of us would have blocked her. Burton opened the envelope, pulled off the rubber band, and extracted the manila folder. He turned the envelope upside down, and the contents fell on the grate of the clean fireplace. He took one of the matches in the container on the mantle and set the contents aflame. He lit fires in four or five places.

"You really should not do that," the police officer said. "I have to tell you that you may be committing a crime." She made no effort to move as she said those words. "I have to tell you that," she said. "I have to warn you that you may face criminal charges."

"It would be a greater crime if anyone read the papers," I said. "Please, let it go."

"I can't stand here and give you permission. That would make me an accessory. If you prevent me from doing my duty — well, there is nothing I could do to stop you, is there?"

"And there is no one to report it, either, is there?" I said.

All of us watched the fire consume the pages. I got a little impatient and didn't want anyone to filch partial pages from the ashes, so I reached down with a poker and spread the flame so that everything burned to ashes.

"My law-officer conscience sometimes argues with my humanitarian conscience," the police officer said. "But you prevented me from doing anything, didn't you?"

"If you have any pangs of conscience," Simon said, "perhaps you'll think about it on the way back to the mainland. There were two murders. Both suspects have confessed. Case closed."

"I never believe in worrying about what might have been." She nodded to her assistant. "Cuff these two, and let's go."

Shortly after the police left, Tonya Borders and Dr. Jeffery Dunn insisted they had to leave immediately. Both of them seemed to have emergency meetings. Lenny Goss and Reginald Ford also demanded that they get out first. Tonya had four large suitcases, and Jeffery had three and a briefcase. Beth Wilson had two large suitcases. Jeffery and Reginald each had to hold suitcases on their laps — which was the only way all five of them could get into the Boston Whaler.

Burton and I said we were in no hurry. Both of us wanted to be back to Atlanta that night. As long as we left by five o'clock we could make it back.

Simon took the others ashore.

Amanda and Simon decided to stay on Palm Island. She would make funeral arrangements. "Jason and I need to be alone for a couple of days," she said. "He and I need to talk and to take all of this in. It's still — well, a shock."

Simon planned to leave as soon as he was sure everything was in order, and he would do what he could. Amanda found a manila file folder in Roger's bedroom. It contained information about Simon's wife, her whereabouts (she was still single), and his two children. As soon as Simon had taken all of us off the island, he planned to phone her.

While we waited for Simon to return, we walked around the small island. It was the first time I had ever seen the entire island in the daytime. The flora amazed me. Peach trees showed their unripened fruit. Black-trunked elms crowded against the sides of the path on the windward side and swayed gently in the wind from the ocean. The aroma of oregano and lemon balm filled our nostrils until we picked up a whiff of honeysuckle and then reached a small bed of roses. Roger must have had at least thirty varieties, and all of them actually smelled as beautiful as they looked. I lost track of the variety of flowers. It was obvious that someone had taken great pains to make it restful. I understood why Simon enjoyed being out there alone.

In the distance we could see the ocean liners that appeared no larger than toys. I turned away and then looked back every few seconds. It was almost as if they got slightly bigger each time.

Amanda brought us a pitcher of iced tea — true Southern style: The tea was weak and very sweet.

"I wish I had known about Roger's change of heart," I said to Burton as we sipped our tea. "When he called me a couple of weeks ago, he did act different. But I didn't think too much about it."

"You're a psychologist," Burton said; "I'm surprised you didn't wonder. I mean, wonder enough to ask or do something."

"He played games with people. I thought it was just another game."

"Yes, I suppose that is the way he was."

"And you know from experience?"

"I know from experience," he said.

I thought Burton was going to open up to me, but just then we heard the Boston Whaler approaching. Roger had a yacht, but he preferred this for guests on the island.

"It takes, what, three minutes to reach shore in the calm waters?"

He shrugged. "Maybe four."

We got into the boat, and just for fun I timed the trip. It was exactly three minutes.

"I'll miss you, Simon," I said after he helped me with my luggage and I gave him a warm hug.

Burton hugged him, as well. "What do you plan to do now?"

He shrugged.

I laughed, and then Burton laughed. It took a few seconds for Simon to catch on.

"The shrug, huh? Oh yes, I do that extremely well. For a moment, I forgot." He gave me another warm hug. "My answer is that I'm not sure. I've saved my money — what is there to spend money on around here? My former wife wants to think about a reconciliation. I believe she'll say yes. I believe that because God has kept love in her heart alive during the years of our separation. She just wants to be sure. I won't make any significant change until I hear from her."

"I'll pray for you and for her every day," Burton said. "What's her name?"

"Sheila," he said.

"Every day, you will be in my prayers."

"I don't know if God listens to me, Simon," I said, "but I'll talk to him regularly about you and Sheila. That's the best I can do."

"Is start." He burst into laughter. "That has been like performing for the tourists. I'll miss the playacting."

We thanked him again and headed for our cars.

"How about coffee?" Burton asked just before I got into my car.

"I thought you'd never ask."

We walked from the pier to the nearest restaurant — about half a mile away. Neither of us seemed to know what to say along the way. I marveled again at the sand dunes and the countless rows of sea oats. Everything smelled fresh, and the sun warmed my arms.

After we sat down and had our coffee served, I said, "You and Simon are the first Christians I've found attractive."

"What kind of Christians have you known?"

"I lived with an uncle and aunt for six months when I was in college — six months before they kicked me out. They had so many 'don't rules,' I finally made a huge poster listing all those rules and hung it in the hallway outside my door. I think I listed fifteen things I couldn't do."

"Is that when they kicked you out?"

"No. As a matter of fact, they liked it. My uncle was sure I was beginning to learn."

"Oh oh. That doesn't sound good."

"They got the message when I put up the next poster."

Burton smiled. "I gotta hear this."

"The first poster said, 'THESE ARE THE THINGS GOOD CHRISTIANS CAN'T DO.'

On the other I wrote, 'THESE ARE THE THINGS GOOD CHRISTIANS CAN DO.' "

"And what did you write under that?"

"Nothing. I left it blank. The next day Uncle Ed asked, 'When are you going to finish the poster?' I answered, 'As soon as I can think of something to put there.' "

"And what happened? Did he fill it in for you?"

"Oh no. He yelled at me. That's all it took."

"Wait — you lost me."

"Sorry." I sipped my coffee. "You see, one of the rules was 'Christians can't get angry.' When he yelled, I pointed to the rule and said, 'You can't do that!' "

"And then — ?"

"He really yelled and told me to get out at the end of the week. But I had the last word."

"Am I supposed to be surprised at that?" Burton showed those gorgeous teeth, and the light was perfect and his dimples glowed, as well.

"I said, 'Uncle Ed, I'm sorry, but I can't do that.' When he asked why, I said, 'Because I don't plan to stay that long. I'll be gone tonight.' Guess what? I never saw him again. But anytime anyone talked to me about the church or Jesus or being a Christian, I thought of him."

"I'm sorry about that —"

"I should have added, until I met you and Simon. You two guys are genuine."

"We try to be."

We both sipped our coffee and looked out the window. The day had grown extremely warm. We sat outside where the soft Atlantic wind could caress our skin. It messed up my hair. No matter how windblown Burton's hair, those curls never looked bad. Why do some guys have all the good hair?

From inside, the aroma of smoking fish filled our nostrils. I thought about food — as usual — but I didn't want to ruin the ambience.

"I want to ask you something," I said and broke the silence.

"Ask," he said. The way he answered made me realize he already knew my question.

"You had a secret, too. Most of the others told theirs, but you didn't."

"And the question is — ?"

"Would you tell me — trust me — with the secret?"

"You're a therapist," he said slowly. He wrapped his hands around his cup and stared into the coffee. "You know there's a time for people to open up."

"We like to say that they'll open up when

they feel safe."

"True," he said, "but it's more than safety. I still have a couple of things to work out within myself first. I hope you'll understand that — as a therapist and as a potential friend."

"As a potential convert," I said. I smiled to deflect my disappointment.

"It's not easy for me to open up," he said. "But I will — eventually."

"I am disappointed, but I'll wait."

"In the meantime," Burton said, "I'd love to talk to you about the Christian faith."

"Again, I thought you'd never ask."

"You're serious? You'd really like to talk about God?"

"I'm serious. This time. Honest," I said, and I meant it. "As I told you earlier, I never met any real Christians before —"

"Or maybe you weren't ready to meet real Christians. Maybe you let a few of the odd ones scare you away from opening up."

I laughed. He had me, and he knew it.

"There is a Sufi saying, and maybe you know it: 'When the pupil is ready, the teacher appears.' "

"That's not fair," I said. "I quote that to clients all the time. In fact, I even have a lovely poster of that on my office wall that one of my appreciative clients made for me."

"Maybe it's time for someone to quote those words to you — and for you to listen."

"Okay, teacher, I want to be a ready pupil. Truly. I mean that."

He leaned forward. "I know you do."

"Isn't this the time where you grab me and kiss me and —"

"Not yet. One day, maybe. Not yet."

"I can wait. I can be patient, too."

"It will also give me a chance to know you better."

"I'm counting on that, as well."

"After we get back to Atlanta," Burton said, "may I take you to dinner one night?"

"Do you take all inquirers to dinner?"

"No, not all," he said and smiled. "Only two kinds."

"Oh? Who are they?"

"Serious males and women with red hair."

"Titian."

"What are you saying?"

"My hair. It's not red. It's titian."

"Okay, I'll amend that to say serious males and titian-haired women."

"In that case, I'm always free on Tuesday evenings."

ABOUT THE AUTHOR

Cecil ("Cec") Murphey has written or cowritten more than one hundred books. Among them are the international bestsellers *Gifted Hands,* which he wrote for Dr. Ben Carson, and *90 Minutes in Heaven,* written for Don Piper.

Cec and his wife, Shirley, live in Atlanta. He would love to hear from readers at www .cecilmurphey.com.

The employees of Thorndike Press hope you have enjoyed this Large Print book. All our Thorndike, Wheeler, and Kennebec Large Print titles are designed for easy reading, and all our books are made to last. Other Thorndike Press Large Print books are available at your library, through selected bookstores, or directly from us.

For information about titles, please call:
(800) 223-1244

or visit our Web site at:
http://gale.cengage.com/thorndike

To share your comments, please write:
Publisher
Thorndike Press
295 Kennedy Memorial Drive
Waterville, ME 04901